MOURNING LARK

Goddess Durga
Book Three

Jen Pretty

In a word, I was too cowardly to do what I knew to be right, as I had been too cowardly to avoid doing what I knew to be wrong.

–CHARLES DICKENS,
GREAT EXPECTATIONS

CHAPTER ONE

The streets were dull and tired. The moon glowed between the black clouds that had been threatening rain all night.

"Can we go home now? We have been out here all night," Drew complained. He was lagging. Durga kept pushing at me mentally, but I knew it wasn't to look for rogue vampires in this city. She had a different target in mind — one who had been suspiciously absent for too long.

"Fine, let's head back to the van," I said, scanning the dark streets one last time.

Singh swung around and marched down the street. He had been dragging his feet too. Interesting that he found energy when we turned for home. His desires rarely went past sleeping and eating now that the city was quiet.

After I killed Frankie's father and Vincent disappeared, our hands had been full with hunting vampires. Vincent spent centuries keeping order in the city, and when he left, there was a big influx of vampires who thought they could get away with whatever they wanted.

They quickly learned Vlad was just as tough if not tougher and Durga took no prisoners. Literally.

We hadn't found a single rogue or fallen vampire in weeks.

Halfway back to the van, the clouds let go of the heavy rain they had been holding. Singh and Drew jogged the rest of the way, but I kept the same pace. The rain cooled my face, hanging off my eyelashes for a moment before dripping to run down my cheeks. It trickled through the seams of my jacket until my shirt clung to my shoulders beneath it.

The van pulled up beside me, and I slid the door open. Singh had shifted into a lion and draped his furry butt across the back seat. I slammed the door shut again and went around to the passenger side, sliding in with a squeak as my wet leather pants squished across the vinyl seat.

"You know it's been quiet..." Drew said. He had brought up the topic four times this week already.

"I already told you, not yet."

"I'm just saying. We don't need to stay here now. Other teams can handle…"

"Just drive the car," I interrupted. When someone leaves you in the dust with zero contact, it's was weird to go chasing after them.

Back at the mansion, Drew went to the entertainment room where voices were cheering at some sports game on the TV. Singh sauntered up the stairs still in lion form.

"Don't you dare lie in my bed all wet," I called to him. He twitched his tail and turned towards my room. I made a mental note to find clean sheets before I went to bed.

I turned down the hall towards the office. I knocked, I still expected to hear Vincent's voice. Vlad's gentler and more Russian accented, "Come in," wasn't as startling as the first few times I'd heard it through the solid wood door, but it still wasn't right.

"Hey, Vlad, any news?" I asked, sitting down in the chair in front of what used to be Vincent's desk. Vlad had left the decor the same in the room. It was like we were both just holding still until Vincent came back. The same books on the bookshelves and the same uncomfortable tiny couches lined the walls. When I looked at them, it brought back memories that I didn't know how to handle.

"No, but as I keep telling you, don't worry about it. Vampires often go off the radar for a few months and pop back up just as quick. It's like time flies by suddenly, and we don't notice."

I heard this already. It didn't make it easier. I needed to hear from Vincent. As soon as I found out he left, I wanted to chase him down, but then vampires crawled all over the city, and I couldn't go. Now Durga was napping most of the time and only coming out to push at my mind. It was like she was saving up her energy for something.

Probably something I would hate.

"Your warlock was hanging around looking for you," Vlad said with a smile.

Great.

"Did he say what he wanted?" I asked, picking non-existent lint off my pants.

"Nope, he popped in and asked where you were."

"Ok, I'll see you later."

Vlad winked at me. I shook my head. Although it was morning, I wasn't tired so I headed for the front door of the mansion. As I entered the foyer, the door swung open, and a smiling Trevor bounced in.

"Hey, Lark," he said. His cheeks had colour to them, and he didn't need to wear baggy clothes to cover his skeletal frame anymore. He was thin, but gaining lean muscle from yoga and the kickboxing the hunters were teaching him.

"Hey, how was school?" I asked

"Pretty good, you leaving?" he hooked his thumb over his shoulder.

"Yeah, I'm just going out for a bit, I'll be back later for our movie," I replied. We had started a ritual movie time in the middle of the day since I didn't need to sleep all day anymore.

"Ok, see you later!" Trevor said as he skipped off.

I walked out the door and went down to the garage to find my SUV.

I pulled into the dusty parking lot in front of The Crossroads bar, where all the witches and warlocks of Frankie's coven hung out, and turned off the SUV, stepping out into the cool morning air. It was an unseasonably cold winter. Nothing like up north, but cool enough that I welcomed the sun that peeked over the horizon bringing a tiny ray of warmth.

I pushed the door open to a full house of witches and warlocks. Every magical head turned to look at me, and the busy room dropped to silence.

Several of the coven members scurried out the back door. A group of witches near me leaned away like I had the plague.

Frankie had visited me at the mansion a couple of times in the last few months, but I hadn't been to their bar. I only now realized that was weird and maybe there was a reason for it.

"Lark," Frankie said.

He waved me into his office. I walked past all the worried faces and into his office, closing the door behind me. Photos still covered the walls, but the pictures with Frankie's father were absent, replaced with newer photos. Frankie pulled me into a hug and held me for a moment, but I pushed him back.

"They are afraid of me?" I asked. "Why are they afraid of me, Frankie?"

He sighed, like the weight of the world rested on his shoulders. "Because you turned into Durga and killed Bennet, Lark. They are all worried that Durga will think they are evil and kill them."

I laughed, but there was no humour in it. "But you aren't afraid that Durga will kill you?"

"No. I think she knows who I am by now," he said with a cocky smile.

"Well, can't you explain it to them?" It was bad enough a few of the vampires in the mansion still avoided me if all the witches and warlocks were afraid of me too?

"I've tried Lark." he sighed again and threw his hands in the air. A helpless gesture. "I think they need more time. Why don't we go out somewhere?"

"I don't feel like going out anywhere," I said, turning to leave.

"Please, Lark? This is a temporary problem. Don't run away from me."

"I'm not running away. I'm just tired suddenly."

Frankie grabbed my hand as I went to turn away and pulled me back to his arms.

"I miss you, Lark. I never see you anymore," he complained, brushing the hair back from my face.

His hair was shaggy, and his beard had a few days growth on it making him look more rugged than usual. His tall frame dwarfed me. He made me feel sheltered from the storm when I was in his arms. It was nice and sweet. It made me forget Vincent for a few minutes.

His eyes locked on mine and I realized I had wandered into thoughts of Vincent while Frankie held me.

"I'm sorry," I whispered.

He kissed my forehead and then let me go, returning to his desk. He always had work to do.

"Yeah, I have a lot of work to do now that my coven is smaller. I have no one who can do the books," he replied to my unspoken thought without looking up.

I was making it worse. Keeping my thoughts under control was impossible. "I'm gonna go," I tried to turn again, but he popped up in front of me.

"Wait, I'm sorry, Lark. I'm just stressed out. It's not your fault. I'll stop reading your mind, ok?"

I snorted a laugh.

"OK," Frankie laughed too. "I'll stop taking what you think so personally."

Doing something fun with Frankie might help me forget my problems, but I was just in a weird mood, and it wouldn't be good for either of us.

"I'll see you tomorrow, OK?"

He bit his lip and nodded. "I'll see you tomorrow, Lark." He leaned in and kissed my lips softly making my heart flutter and do foolish things. His hand came around my back, sliding up my spine and the sweet kiss turned into more. Time stood still, and I got completely lost in the moment. When we both came up for air, I laughed. That was one thing Frankie and I were always on the same page about. He hugged me and then I walked back out through the now empty bar and into the morning light.

The drive back to the house was lonely. I was tired of feeling so alone.

Back at the mansion, I struggled to remember feeling lonely while pinned under a 400lb lion and wedged between two laughing hyenas. Ok, the hyenas were Trevor and Drew. They had chosen a comedy for movie time, and it was hilarious. Even my crappy mood couldn't stop every bubble of laughter that lurched out of me. When it was over, the three of us worked together to roll Singh off, and we went to the kitchen to grab lunch.

"That was a good movie. We could watch the sequel tomorrow," Trevor said.

"Great idea," Drew agreed.

They both looked at me for confirmation, but I was considering something else.

"I think it's time to go, actually."

"Go where?" Trevor asked at the same time as Drew said "About time."

"I'm going to go find Vincent," I replied as I stood up and returned my dishes and then went to tell Vlad.

Driving away from the mansion was a little strange. Like a ship set adrift, I somehow knew I wouldn't be back for a while. Durga stirred inside me as if she had read my thought and agreed. When I blinked, her smiling image flashed on the backs of my eyelids. At least she was happy. This new feeling worried me but compelled me forward faster than the legal limit.

"We have plenty of time, Lark," Drew said, gripping the door handle with white knuckles.

"That doesn't mean I need to drive like a grandma." I took the next turn slower, Drew still braced himself.

"No, but you don't have to drive like we are in a road race, either," he replied.

The speed limit was only a suggestion, and I wasn't going that fast.

I was only bringing Drew and, of course, Singh. The three of us had become inseparable in the last few months. Cedric had taken over some duties at the house to help Vlad, so we barely saw him anymore.

Drew gasped as I went through a yellow light. It wasn't like he would even die if we crashed. The thought reminded me of Randy's death in the yoga studio explosion. There was maybe a chance Drew would die if I crashed.

I slowed down to the limit, just in case.

"Lark, are we almost there? I'm cramped back here," Singh said. The SUV had plenty of leg room, but Singh spent as much time as possible as a lion these days, so he always felt cramped as a human.

"We'll be there soon. You can stay human a bit longer, you lazy house cat," I said. He growled lowly but stopped complaining. A lion in my back seat would most definitely cause an accident on the highway.

I was as eager to get there as Singh was, though for different reasons. Vaughn, Vincent's twin brother, hadn't seen Vincent, but he had heard reports of their fallen brother Vernon being in the city, so I had hope that Vincent was there too—hunting his brother.

We pulled into the long-term parking lot and walked through the busy airport.

"Gate 7," Drew whispered pointing to the big sign. Vincent's Jet was in Russia, so we were taking a commercial flight. Which meant, checked luggage and customs, but we were flying first class with a suite, thanks to Vincent's little black credit card, so at least we would have privacy and Singh could be his annoying cat self for the twelve-hour flight.

A woman with huge hair and a grumpy face checked our luggage, and we made our way slowly through customs. Finally, we boarded the large plane. I still wasn't over my fear of small aircraft, so the jumbo jet was perfect. An attractive woman in uncomfortable shoes led us to a small room. It wasn't much bigger than the bathroom in my old apartment, but the door locked. Singh sighed as he shifted into a lion. Drew wrestled two of the seats down into an awkward cat bed and Singh was snoring in seconds.

"You want to play cards?" Drew asked.

"Sure,"

He pulled a deck out of his carry-on and shuffled them before dealing.

"Go fish," he said.

I laughed and checked my cards. We played for a while to the soundtrack of Singh snoring. When the buckle seat belts light came on, we paused our game and buckled up for take-off. Singh was still spread eagle across two seats, but I figured he was pretty indestructible and if we hit a bump and he fell off the seat, it would be hilarious. I held my phone at the ready to take a video. It would win the Internet.

CHAPTER TWO

Halfway through our flight, there was a knock at the cabin door. Singh shifted and sat up in his seat.

I unlocked the door and accepted the three trays of food the stewardess handed me. She also brought a bottle of wine which I tucked under my arm. I sat back down in my seat and unscrewed the cap of the wine bottle. Drew held out a glass, but I drank from the bottle.

"Oh, shit," Drew muttered.

"What?" Singh asked.

Drew pointed at me, but Singh just looked confused.

"I forgot you haven't been around Lark when she drinks. How did you miss the last time?" Drew asked.

"He was sleeping in my bed," I supplied helpfully.

"What happens when she drinks?" Singh asked.

"She gets weird and does dumb shit."

"Hey," I said, but he wasn't wrong. I figured if I had six more hours to kill playing cards with Drew while I listened to Singh snore, it was a good time to make it more interesting. Plus, I already felt calmer about seeing Vincent again.

Singh smiled. "This could be fun, then."

"Definitely more fun than staring at your lion bits while you snore away on that seat," I said, taking another swig of my cheap wine.

"No one said you had to look," Singh said indignantly.

I laughed and shuffled the cards.

"At least eat something," Drew said.

I took a bite of the sandwich before wrapping it back up and taking another long drink of the wine. Half the bottle was gone already. I chuckled to myself. Yeah, go fish would get interesting.

I dealt the cards, one of them fell on the floor, and another landed on the half of Singh's sandwich still sitting on his tray.

"What are we playing?" Singh asked.

"Go fish!" I replied, picking up my cards and organizing them into suits. Another guzzle at the bottle of wine and Drew swiped it out of my hands. He chugged a bunch. Thief.

By the second hand, I was lying on the floor tossing my cards up in the air one at a time. They fluttered gracefully to the floor around me or landed on my face, poking me in the eye. The odds were even.

When one stabbed me in the nose, and both my eyes were watering from falling card damage, I dropped my heavy arms down beside me and stared at the plane's ceiling through my watery eyes.

"I think I love him," I said, interrupting Singh and Drew's conversation about some sports thing.

"Who?" Drew asked.

Durga rolled in my stomach, sloshing wine back up my throat but I swallowed it down and soldiered on.

"Vincent," I said. "He is so pretty with his eyes and his jaw and his nose. He looks amazing with his shirt off. I want to eat him up."

The guys were quiet for so long I sat up on my elbows and looked at them. Both wore shocked expressions.

"What?"

Drew shook his head and turned his focus to tidying up his tray and cutlery. I looked at Sing, but he shifted back into a lion and flopped back on his seat bed.

I lay back on the floor and stared at the ceiling some more. Vincent was handsome and smart and funny. He was also an asshole and a total shit head for not calling me. Crap, was I one of those girls that got all clingy when a man lost interest? Nah, I was just drunk. I laughed out loud and Drew looked over at me with concern. I waved him off and curled up in my tiny bit of floor space between the two rows of seats.

Listening to Singh's rhythmic snoring, I must have nodded off, because next thing I knew, Drew was shaking me awake.

"We are about to land. It would be best if you got in your seat," he said.

Grumbling, I heaved myself up. I was stiff and had a kink in my neck from sleeping on the hard floor. My head was pounding. Man, that wine hit me hard.

I buckled in and tried to finger-comb my hair. I found the queen of hearts stuck in my hair and laughed, setting it on the table before catching Singh's eyes. The smile fell from my face as I registered his curious look.

"What is it?" I asked him.

"You shouldn't drink," he said.

Memories floated back. I remembered playing go fish, chasing a dropped card and ending up lying on the floor… Oh shit.

I dropped my head in my hands as I remembered declaring my love for Vincent and vowed never to drink wine again.

"Let's pretend that didn't happen," Drew said, increasing my mortification.

My ears popped as the plane approached the tarmac and I looked out the window to see lights dotting a white cityscape. Snow. Great. I had wrongly assumed it would be warm by this time of year.

As the plane bumped down to a landing, Durga stirred again, and I tossed my senses out to search the city for Vincent. Vampires packed the city. I didn't understand why they would want to live here, but there had to be thousands.

No sign of Vincent, but I found Vaughn. He was across the city. I knew he had a house in the city and Vlad said he would let Vaughn know to expect us.

I brought my senses back in and opened my eyes. The guys were gathering their carry on, so I unbuckled and grabbed mine too. Drew handed me a winter coat and hat and we all dressed for the Russian winter.

I cursed as we walked through the accordion tunnel from the plane to the airport. It wasn't snowy, but it was cold as hell, and I wanted to turn around and go home.

Durga woke up and pressed me forward. I guess we had work to do.

We exited the echoing tunnel into the airport. The terminal was a massive structure of glass and arches. The ceiling was several stories up and gave it the feeling of a vast open space that countered drastically with the press of travelers. We walked past several other gates with lines of people pulling suitcases or carrying small children. A man built like a gladiator stood by the line of doors. He held a sign that said 'Lark.'

"Hi," I said, walking through a group of people who had come in the door.

He spotted me and lowered his sign. "Hello, you are Lark? I drive you to Lord Vaughn." The man had a thick Russian accent.

"All right, sounds good," I said.

He took my bag, and we followed him out into the snowy street of Moscow. At the curb, a black town car waited, engine running. A man got out, and our giant handed him some money and slid into the driver seat. We all climbed in, and the car pulled out into heavy traffic. Most of the streets were one way and a tight fit between parked cars. The white stone buildings stretched up into the sky and hugged the streets, making me feel claustrophobic. When we pulled onto a highway, the vehicle zipped along fast, going in and out of tunnels and switching lanes to avoid other vehicles. It was a real live video game. Before long, the car left the highway and came back onto some smaller streets. The car swung around corners like it was a police chase. Drew's face was pale, and he gripped the seat as if it could save him. I bet he appreciated my driving now. I bit my lip to keep from laughing. Singh fidgeted beside me. I could tell he already wanted to shift back into a lion. He would forget how to be a human if he wasn't careful.

We passed a rounded building that was several stories high and lit up like a Christmas tree.

"What is that?" I asked.

"Is shop," The driver said.

"Like a mall?" Drew asked through clenched teeth, still gripping the door.

"Yes," the man replied, his eyes never leaving the road.

That was a big ass mall. I hoped we would have time to stop in. My hastily packed suitcase didn't have all the necessities. I tried to remember what I had put in. It would be a surprise. The car took us to a quieter area of the city, the streets got cleaner, and there were ornate trees and beautiful landscaping.

The car stopped in front of a gate that slid open revealing a pillared mansion that curved around a courtyard. It was three stories high and made from smooth brick.

The car pulled up to the imposing building and stopped in front of the door. A Human stepped out onto the snow cleared front steps. Vaughn followed him. His face was serious which made him look so much like Vincent I almost thought it was him for a moment, but when I climbed out of the car, his open smile confirmed it was the happier twin. Not the grumpy one I longed to see.

Singh shifted and sauntered past me, taking the stairs in a single leap and then maneuvered himself around the old vampire to enter the mansion. Rude cat.

Vaughn watched him go past then descended the steps to greet me. He took me in his arms and spun me around. It caught me off guard, but when he pulled back smiling at me, I had to smile too. He was contagious.

"Welcome to my home, Lark. I am glad to have you here."

"Thanks. Also, thank you for sending a car to pick us up. Moscow is a beautiful city," I replied. "This is Drew."

"Nice to meet you.

"You too," Drew replied.

"Were you chosen by Durga or Lark?" Vaughn asked with a wicked grin.

"He's on my team. Vincent chose him," I replied.

Vaughn didn't look convinced but let it go. It reminded me of the time Vincent had been yelling at Drew, and I bit his head off. I wasn't sure if it was my voice or Durga's when I told Vincent Drew was "mine."

"Welcome. I hope you enjoy your stay though I know you are not here to be a tourist."

"Thanks, no, but I would like to stay for a little while once I find your brother. Or brothers," I said with a shiver. The cold was permeating my coat. It was almost April; shouldn't it be warmer here? Maybe it was winter all year round. I shivered again.

Vaughn noticed and hustled us into the house where a crackling fire in the large foyer welcomed us. The man who drove us through the city brought our bags in behind us, and the human closed the door, sealing out the frigid cold.

Two vampires I recognized stood in the foyer. They had come with Vaughn on his trip to the US. They were all muscles and scowls until Durga perked up and looked at them from my eyes. She did a flip inside me like she was excited to see them. I bet they would lead to chasing and slaughtering vampires. All Durga's favourite things.

The Russian vampires' postures straightened, as their glowing eyes met my red ones, standing at attention — men ready to serve their new commander. Durga was nearly purring.

I noticed they each had the handle of a short sword sticking up over their shoulder. Durga liked men with weapons too.

"Now, Durga, let's get Lark, and your friends settled before you fall back into your old games," Vaughn chuckled.

Durga relented and let my eyes bleed back to normal.

"What does that mean?" I asked.

"Come and sit down and I'll tell you a story," Vaughn said before turning down a hall papered in antique velvet wallpaper. The hardwood floors tapped under our feet as we shuffled further into the mansion. There were arches above every door along the hall, and when Vaughn opened one, it led to a beautiful sitting room with 15-foot ceilings and full-length windows that overlooked a garden.

The two vampires from the foyer had followed too and were standing flanking the door like personal security guards.

"Do you need security in the house?" I asked.

Vaughn chuckled. "They saw Durga in your eyes. They won't soon relax. She was with us once as you know. Durga chose these two herself. They were the best soldiers of the time, Gladiators. Durga started the first hunter team and trained them herself. They have been working for me since she left us."

I absorbed that information. This man knew way more about Durga than what was in the book.

"Why don't I know this stuff?" I asked.

"Durga warned me not to tell her future incarnations about it. The fact she is still in remission tells me she doesn't mind if I tell you everything."

My eyes flashed red again.

"Ok, maybe not everything." Vaughn laughed sitting down in an armchair.

My vision cleared, and I took a seat with Drew on a plush sofa. At least Vaughn had comfortable furniture in his office, unlike Vincent and his hard couch.

I had a feeling that Vaughn and Durga had more than a passing relationship. Her reaction confirmed it and made me uncomfortable. It was as if Vaughn knew personal things about me even though it wasn't me he knew. Durga was becoming more and more a part of me, like a past I had forgotten. I fidgeted under Vaughn's gaze.

"So, you haven't heard from Vincent either?" Drew asked, drawing Vaughn's attention. I knew I liked Drew for a reason.

Vaughn sighed. "No, I haven't heard about him being anywhere else though. He fell off the map not long after he arrived here. If he was in the tunnels, I would have heard.

"The tunnels?" I asked.

"Most of the vampires live in the abandoned tunnels beneath the city. It's a large system of old, defunct mines, sewers and tunnels dug by vampires centuries ago connecting them all to an underground world that is purely of vampire design. Many things go on down there. Long ago it was overrun with fallen and rogue vampires who used the system to evade Durga's wrath. My teams patrol it now to keep it free of unwelcome types, but I will warn you, it's not a nice place. I allow more rope than Vincent did in his city. Of course, I remove those who kill humans, but many vampires relish a more… alternative lifestyle."

I raised an eyebrow. "Alternative?"

He smiled. "Nothing I am interested in, but to each their own."

I didn't need to hear more about that. I would find Vincent and not have to spend any time in dark tunnels.

"So, do you have any suggestions on where we should look for Vincent?" Drew asked.

I mentally begged he wouldn't say the tunnels.

"The tunnels," he replied, picking lint off his pant leg.

Fuck.

CHAPTER THREE

"All right, so tell me more about Durga and the muscle by the door," I said trying to keep the thought of dark, damp tunnels out of my mind.

Vaughn smiled and looked over at them. "The one on the right is Vilen." The man nodded once, his eyes holding mine. "And the other is Ninel." The second man nodded as well but kept his eyes on the floor. Durga flashed a vision of Ninel as a human slumped before us, bloody and broken. His arm was almost severed at the shoulder, and half his face was a pulpy mess. His lungs pulled great gulps of air but only one eye shone up at us, the other was just an empty hole. Our hand reached out and laid upon his head. It wasn't my hand, but I knew it was Durga. We healed Ninel as we had done with Singh in the bar after the battle with Frankie's father.

"You look well," she spoke, using my voice and Ninel fell to a knee. He bowed his head down. "Rise warrior. We will battle together soon. Blood will run like rivers." Durga snapped back into her quiet place inside me as Ninel rose and lifted his eyes to meet me. They hadn't acted like this when Durga was only a stirring inside me. We were different now. She and I were one.

"She comes and goes as she pleases?" Vaughn asked.

"Yes, but we work together. She doesn't push me out of the way as much anymore," I said.

"That is so interesting. When she was here last, over two centuries ago, she used to block out Elianna. The girl never knew what happened unless I told her. Durga frowned upon it though. I think she tried to save the girl from the horrors of the battles."

"She did that for a while. It didn't work for either of us though."

He nodded, considering the information.

"Well, should I show you to your room? I'm sure you are eager to get out and look for Vincent." He smiled and stood, then walked past the two Muscle-bound men by the door. Drew and I followed along behind him, but as soon as I was through the door, the two men turned and followed me, leaving Drew to tag along behind them.

I looked back and caught glimpses of Drew as he marched behind. It seemed they established the pecking order. Drew looked happy to follow, so I left it alone. Durga purred in pleasure at the wall of muscle at my back. Vilen held my eye and lifted one side of his mouth in a smile. Cocky. Durga liked that and batted her red eyes at him. I turned back to watch where I was going. I would not fall and embarrass myself because Durga wanted to make dough eyes at the giant man.

Vaughn led us upstairs and to a room with a snoring lion on the bed. Vilen set my bag down on the chair in the corner and then stepped back to flank the door.

I cleared my throat, startling the lion, but he grumbled and rolled onto his back. Great.

I turned to face Vaughn. "Thank you for letting us stay here. I think I'll get changed and then we will head out to get looking. I haven't been able to sense Vincent, but I'll try again before I go."

Vaughn nodded and handed me a cell phone and a credit card.

"I have a credit card," I explained.

I would disappoint Vincent if I didn't make sure you had everything you needed. Sometimes American cards do not work in stores. This one will be better for Russia."

"Ok, thanks," I took the items. I needed the phone. Mine quit somewhere over the north pole. I guess I didn't have international roaming set up.

"I have put my number in the address book along with Vilen and Ninel's, though I doubt they will be far enough you will need to call for them on the phone."

With that somewhat ominous statement, Vaughn left, closing the door behind him and sealing me in with a sleeping lion, a weird surfer dude and two slabs of Russian muscle.

The room was plain, other than the fact it contained our odd team of vampire hunters. White walls and beige bedding dotted with white cat hair.

I grabbed my bag and went to the washroom to have a quick shower and change into clean clothes I hadn't been rolling around on the ground in an airplane wearing.

I shut the door behind me and heard the Russians move to stand in front. The Tv flicked on, and the sound of someone speaking Russian slid under the door as I rooted through my bag. I had a sweater and a pair of shorts: six pairs of socks, no clean underwear and one running shoe. Fuck my life. Good thing I had a credit card.

I took a shower and washed my hair, then combed the tangles out with a brush I found in the drawer beside the sink. When I reemerged, cleaner and less funky, Drew scooted past the giants into the bathroom too, carrying his bag. Vilen and Ninel moved back to the main door. I wondered if all they did was guard doors.

Durga took that moment to show me what they could do.

The two Russians were swinging swords and decapitating advancing hordes of vampires. Their muscles bulged and rippled as their weapons sliced through the air with a whistle. Each back swing sprayed blood through the air, and their grunts filled the air as the chopped down dozens and dozens of ravenous fallen vampires.

Durga dropped me out of the vision so fast, I almost collapsed. Well, note to self, don't piss off the Russian vampires. They were warriors all right.

I collapsed on the bed next to Singh. I was sure Durga was leaving me the hangover as a lesson in the consequences of drinking. She was a bitch sometimes. I closed my eyes and rubbed my forehead.

There was no warning before a sandpaper tongue slid up the side of my face, scratching and drooling all over me.

"Gross, Singh. What is wrong with you?"

He huffed a few times like a lion version of a laugh. As Drew exited the bathroom, hair still dripping and in clean clothes, Singh rolled up and hopped down off the bed, before stretching like a cat and then sauntering into the bathroom, slamming the door behind him.

"MNE NE NRAVITSYA LEV," Vilen said.

"What's that?" I asked from the bed, looking up at the Russian.

"I am not sure I like this lion," he said.

"You and me both," I said laughing.

"Don't provoke him," Drew warned.

There was a roar from the bathroom.

"Well then stop being such a dink, Singh," I yelled in reply. You would think he would have thicker skin, being a lion and all, but he was sensitive, often stomping off in a huff if I poked fun at him.

I sat up in the middle of the bed and tried to use my sense to find Vincent again. Searching the city I found a lot of vampires again, but even as I tried to focus in on Vincent, I couldn't sense him at all.

He came back out a few minutes later in human form and dressed in clean clothes. He gave me a scathing glare and then pulled on his boots. I got up and tracked down my winter clothes I had tossed on the couch that ran along one wall, then we all marched down to the main foyer where the house human was waiting.

He reminded me of Drake, Vincent's house manager, killed by the rogues. Maybe anyone who gave their lives to serve vampires had to be a certain type of person.

"BLAGODARYU VAS," Vilen said as the human handed him a set of keys. Vilen then opened the door and held it for me. I walked through, but a scuffle behind me made me turn back. Singh had shifted and had Vilen by the throat. When Vilen went limp, Singh walked over the Russian man and out the door to sidle up. He rubbed his furry head on my stomach and purred.

"You could have used your words," I said, petting the bad cat anyway. Vilen stood up and dusted off his pants, then nodded once to the lion and we were all a happy family again. Vilen's neck was whole and unmaimed. Having seen what Singh could do, his restraint impressed me. The big cat licked my hand and rubbed one more time across my stomach. Pecking order established now, we all crammed into a Hummer parked in the driveway as the gate to Vaughn's mansion slid open.

"Where would you like to start?" Vilen asked from behind the wheel.

"I need to get clothes. Let's start there. If we have to go into the sewer, I will need waterproof boots too." I looked down at Drew's boots. He would need some too.

I couldn't believe we were going down in the sewers like the freaking ninja turtles.

The hummer sailed through the city, past some incredible architecture and pulled into a parking space in front of a glass building. We all piled out, and Vilen pointed to what looked like a blocked off-road. People moved in and out between the posts that blocked out traffic.

"Mall in Red Square," Vilen declared with a look like he had single-handedly saved the day.

"Thanks," I said, moving past him across the street and down a narrow alley beside what turned out to be the state museum into a long wide courtyard. Hundreds of people walked around here — tourists with cameras and cell phones taking photos of the buildings and scenery. The building that Vilen pointed to was a castle. It would still hold out to an army attack. The stone walls looked ancient. I glanced towards the end of the Red Square and saw the stunning Saint Basil Cathedral. It looked like it belonged in a theme park — colourful turrets and spires, topped with gumdrops in green and red and gold stripes and patterns. I had never seen anything so beautiful and filled with history. I hoped we would have time to tour the buildings in the Red Square before I left.

Wind swept through the square, chilling me to the bone and pushing me into the giant mall. Once I was inside the design of the old structure again struck me. I could see clear up to the sky through the arched glass ceiling several stories above. Escalators carried people up and down to the various floors of food, clothing and all manner of things.

"Can you find me a clothing store?" I asked Vilen. The place was huge. I would be here all day. He nodded and took us on a tour of the building, going up three floors and walking along the glass balcony railing, we weaved through the other shoppers and teenagers mulling about. We even passed a group of senior women who were striding along at a brisk pace. We came to a halt just inside the doors of a department store.

"Perfect," I said as I walked into the women's clothing section, Singh and Drew went to the men's department on the other side of the aisle. Vilen and Ninel followed me around as I grabbed pants and shirts and underwear. That wasn't awkward at all. I went to the back of the store and found the shoe section, selected some tall rubber boots and tossed it all into a shopping cart that Ninel had procured from somewhere. Singh and Drew caught up to us at the cash register. I put all of our items on Vaughn's credit card.

"I got these for you," Drew said, holding up a pair of waterproof pants. That was a smart idea.

"Thanks, Drew." I smiled at him, and he nodded.

The woman behind the cash spoke in Russian. I assumed it was how much I owed her, so I handed her Vaughn's credit card, and she seemed happy enough with that.

We were all set. We left the department store each carrying two bags. I admit most of the items were mine, but that happens with you pack in two seconds and dash out the door on a crazy mission to find a guy who has ghosted you.

I stopped walking, struck stupid by that thought. What if he was taking a vacation? I had brought a lot of drama into Vincent's life. He left me a letter and took off.

"Lark," It was Drew, he stood at my shoulder looking around like we were just enjoying the scenery. "What's up?"

"He doesn't want me to find him?" I said.

"How do you know?" he asked.

I thought about it for a moment. I didn't know that. But what if this was all a huge mistake and when I found him, he was angry or worse, didn't care?

"I haven't known Vincent that long, but I don't think it's in his character to just drop off the face of the earth, do you?"

I shook my head.

"Then let's go find him, ok?"

I nodded and took a step forward. Everyone else walked again too, but Ninel kept glancing back at me. Not meeting my eye, but more like he was making sure I was following. Vilen just continued his scanning of our surroundings. He was full security guard all the time.

My mind kept slipping back to thoughts of Vincent. Would he be upset I came? Durga reminded me of the time I walked in to see him drinking from a tall blond woman. Stupid Deity. She was the worst bff in history. I pushed them all out of my mind. I was here to catch Vernon; get him for all the pain and suffering. For blowing up the vampires in Canada and for killing Randy and my Yoga studio. I was here for revenge. Not to get some guy.

Ok, I was here a little bit to get the guy. Whatever. Oh my God. I needed to stop. New brain, please?

We got back to the hummer and tossed all the stuff in the back.

Ready or not, it was time to see about some sewage tunnels.

CHAPTER FOUR

We drove through the city; I didn't know where we were going, but leaned back in my seat and closed my eyes to search for Vincent again. It was no use. Either he wasn’t here, or my tracking was on the fritz. I wanted to believe it was the latter. If he wasn't here, there was a whole world I would have to search.

I opened my eyes, realizing the hummer had stopped and everyone was just sitting there waiting for me.

“Let's go,” I said.

We gathered our new rubber boots, waterproof gear and flashlights. At least someone was thinking ahead. I had forgotten flashlights.

When we were all geared up, Vilen grabbed a crowbar from under the seat in the hummer and shut the trunk. He locked the doors, and we followed him and his ominous crowbar to a back alley where he popped off the sewer drainage grate, uncovering a deep dark hole into the underbelly of Moscow.

Singh descended first, followed by Ninel and then Vilen waved me down while he held the grate. I placed my foot carefully on each rung of the ladder. My boots squeaked on the old steel, and I gripped tighter. It was twenty feet before I splashed down into a puddle of something, I didn't think too hard about. Ninel was watching down the tunnel while Drew held his flashlight so I could see what I was doing.

"Thanks," I said when he pulled an extra flashlight out of his pocket and handed it to me. The ceiling in the tunnel was high. I hoped it wasn't because the city experienced a lot of flooding. I was not ok with swimming in these temperatures though it was warmer in the sewer than on the street.

Once we were all in the sewer, Ninel led the way on a twisting tour through the underground. We came out of the narrow sewer into an old subway station. A ticket booth still stood at the bottom of a set of wide stairs, though the stairs had been bricked off. There was dust on the ground, but otherwise, the platform area was pristine.

Ninel pressed in one of the bricks, and a doorway opened in the wall, leading into another platform, crowded with people. Not people, Vampires.

We walked through, and the door swung shut. Music echoed through the hollow underground room. Its fast beat matched the vampires dance as they lurched and shook around each other. I noticed humans in the mix. Durga stirred inside me, unhappy with the humans being in here with so many vampires. Coloured lights shone out of recessed pot lights in the ceiling high above, but other than the cement walls, it was set up like a nightclub.

"We keep the balance, Durga," Ninel said. His voice didn't have such a deep accent. It shocked me in its softness.

I could only see half his face as the other half was in shadows, but it reminded me of the flash Durga had sent me of the man destroyer. Durga came to the surface and reached out to lay her hand on his face, cupping his cheek. The coloured lights turned a shade of red as she took over control of my body and spoke to the vampire. The loud beat of the music seemed to fade away as the world slowed down and only Ninel was in focus. The look on his face spoke of centuries of camaraderie and companionship. It felt like a homecoming.
It was almost uncomfortable to witness, like a private moment that I wasn't a part of.

"You have always kept the balance. I am proud of you, Ninel."

Ninel let out a ragged breath and tipped his head into my hand.

I would need to hear this story. There was more to Ninel and Durga than they told me. Durga's image flashed on the back of my eyelids and nodded before she settled in her place, and I looked at Ninel through my normal eyes. I went to drop my hand, but before I could, he put his hand on mine and pressed a kiss to my palm. Then he turned away and surveyed the underground nightclub.

Still in shock, I watched his profile for a minute before a purring rumble alerted me to Singh, as a lion, standing close beside me. The vampires closest to us noticed him and pushed away into the crowd, but soon every vampire in the place was staring at us, and the music stopped. We were standing in silence, flashing lights zipping across the crowd.

"Hey there," I said, waving.

Singh moved forward and parted the crowd. I followed behind him, and he led me up to a table where the DJ had been playing records. Singh shifted and grabbed a microphone. He flicked it on and blew into it. The loud feedback that made everyone cover their ears.

“Oops, sorry about that,” he said into the microphone. “Here is your Goddess. She has a few words to say.”

I scowled at the lion. I didn’t have things to say to anyone. He shoved the microphone in my hand and nodded towards the crowd.

I turned around, and they were all waiting for me to speak. Fuck.

“Hi there,” I said too closely to the microphone. More feedback rang through the echoing chamber. “Sorry, look, I'm just trying to find Vincent. He looks exactly like Vaughn. You all know who he is?” There were affirmative replies and heads nodding. I didn’t know much Russian, but it seemed like they knew enough English I got my point across. I gave them a thumbs up and set the microphone down on the DJ table. It rang a loud squeal through the room and Singh grabbed it up and flicked it off before setting it down again.

“Sorry,” I said again as I followed Singh back through the crowd to where the team stood. Drew gave me a double thumbs up. Great, that probably meant I made a fool of myself.

“Come on, Lark. Let's go look around the tunnels, huh?” Drew said. He was way too keen to be down here. I sighed and followed behind them as we moved along the wall. The music started back up again, but most people kept watching us until we were out of sight. We took another quick turn, and the sounds faded, except for the splashing of our boots in the water that trickled along the same direction we were going. They made the walls in this tunnel of red brick and mortar. It curved above us, well beyond my reach, but Vilen had hunched so his head wouldn't hit any of the hanging ice stalactites.

We walked along for miles, it seemed. The sound of our boots splashing through the water and the vague scent of scum assaulted my senses. As we walked, my neck prickled like someone was watching me. I glanced over my shoulder, but there was no one behind us.

"What is it?" Drew asked.

"Nothing," I replied.

The tunnel narrowed until we had to walk single file, splashing along through the little stream of water at our feet.

The second time I felt someone watching me, I spun back abruptly. There was still no one there.

"What's wrong?" Drew asked.

I put my finger to my lips, and I sent out my senses. Someone was there. A vampire. Just beyond the bend. I pointed back to the last corner we had turned. Vilen had to lift me to get past in the narrow space. He set me back down and crept back towards the turn. The puddle at our feet should have splashed and sloshed under his steps, but it was silent.

He had turned into a hunter. Stealthy and focused, he stopped at the corner.

Singh moved in beside me, pressing me into the wall of the tunnel with his giant head. His thick mane tickled my hand, and I shivered at the rumble of his silent growl.

In one swift movement, Vilen swung around the corner, and the spy squeaked like a stepped-on Pomeranian. Vilen came back around the corner and stomped through the slosh of water carrying a skinny vampire by the front of his coat. His feet held off the ground, the vampire squirmed and mewled. Vilen set his captive back on his feet and turned him, so he faced me.

The vampire had spiked hair and his legs, clad in skinny jeans, looked like toothpicks below his heavy coat. His eyes fell on me, and he took a step forward, raising his hand like he would touch my face.

Singh growled at his boldness, and he took a step back, raising his hands in a placating gesture. "I'm sorry. Don't eat me."

Durga pushed forward and had a look at him, then sunk back. She rarely took an interest unless someone had been breaking her laws, so I took a second look at the weird skinny vampire. He wasn't thin the way Trevor had been. It was more like this vampire just moved so much. He burned off his meals. He stood there fidgeting and shifting from foot to foot.

"What do you want?" I asked. Singh rubbed his face on my stomach again, like he was marking me as his. I tried to push him away, but that just made him lick my hands, so I gave up and let him rub his damn head on me.

"I just… uhm. This will sound strange." The spike-haired vampire was fidgeting twice as much now. Scratching his neck, biting his nails, tapping out a rhythm in the puddle under his feet.

"Spill it," I said.

The nervous vampire startled. "I saw a witch once. She told me to look for you. That I would crown the king. That's what she said. I would crown the king and save the Lark. Crown the king, save the Lark. See I remembered it all this time."

"What's the matter with you?" I asked.

"I've been waiting here a very, very long time."

Of course, Drew could be counted on to ask the question I wasn't sure I wanted to know the answer to.

"How long?" Drew asked.

"243 years," he said, smiling. He looked kind of demented when he smiled. His fangs were a yellow colour instead for the white of normal vampires. I wished he would stop, but he kept on smiling.

Vilen stepped up behind the sketchy vampire and put his hand on the smaller man's shoulder.

"What's your name?" I asked.

The vampire looked back at me, calmer now. Like having Vilen's hand on him had grounded him and made him more normal. "My name is Alex."

"How are you doing that?" I asked Vilen. I wasn't sure he was doing anything. But Alex stood quietly, his arms at his sides and a relaxed look on his face.

"He is sketched. Has been out of direct contact with another vampire for too long. He needs to hold hand for a while," Vilen said with a hearty chuckle.

"There are plenty of vampires down here," I said.

"They don't like me much," Alex said leaning towards Vilen.

"Why is that?" I asked against my better judgment. I was sure I wouldn't want to know the answer to that one.

"Because I will save the Lark and crown the king." He smiled again, but now it was a sleepy smile.

"Am I collecting vampires now? This is ridiculous. Wait, what are you doing?" Vilen had picked up the smaller vampire and tossed him over his shoulder.

"We take home sketched vampire," Vilen said.

"If he is telling the truth, he will save your life, Lark," Drew said. "We both know those powerful witches see things. Besides, if he waited here all those years, you can't leave him behind, can you?" Jerk. He knew I couldn't stand a sob story like that. This vamp was another stray for my collection. Durga pressed forward and used my tongue to speak.

"He is mine," she declared and retreated again. I was tired of her popping in and out, and I expressed my displeasure by giving her a shove. She didn't care. I was sure I couldn't hurt the ancient deity that lived inside me. I imagined I could sometimes. It brought a smile to my face.

The waterproof pants were brilliant. I was still dry. The narrow tunnel went on for miles but eventually opened into what seemed to be a bunker. Vampires were laying on bunk beds or sitting on old sofas that must have been carried down through the tunnels. Alex, who had been doing an impression of a dead person, looked up. He patted Vilen's arm, and Vilen set him on his feet.

"Look guys! I found the Lark!" He said to the vampires in the room. Then he held out his hands towards me like I was the top prize on a game show.

"Holy shit," one of them whispered. The rest sat up and stared at me like I was a ghost.

"I'm looking for someone,' I said. "He looks like Vaughn, your city leader."

After some head shaking and mumbled apologies, I sighed and turned to go. This was a bust.

"You check Metro two?" A Russian voice called from the back.

"You can't get in there anymore. It's a myth," Alex called back.

"Not myth," grumbled the same voice.

"What is Metro two?" I asked.

"It's government tunnels. Everyone knows someone who says they know someone who can get in, but it's sealed up. It's impossible to get in," Alex replied.

One thing Vincent had taught me, nothing was impossible if you knew the right people and had enough money.

"Ok, let's get out of here. I'm freezing my ass off," I said.

"I know a shortcut," Alex said, trotting off in the opposite direction from which we had come. Tugging my coat close around my neck, we strode off after the eccentric vampire.

CHAPTER FIVE

After sloshing through several more tunnels and one bit of climbing, we were back on the streets of Moscow, but not anywhere near the hummer.

"This way, we take metro," Vilen said.

That is how I found myself standing on an ornate underground platform, with hundreds of other people, a twitchy vampire and an impatient lion man in human form.

Singh paced the edge, past the line painted on the cement that warned of danger. Bored looking commuters and gawking tourists packed the platform behind us. The pillars supporting the ceiling were arched and the floor was tiled like a chess board, not that I could see much of it under the horde of pedestrian feet. Looking up, the vaulted ceiling was reminiscent of a cathedral. Giant chandeliers hung from the top and ornate stucco designs were carved and painted all the way down the platform. It seemed to go on for miles.

"Traffic is light right now," Ninel said.

"Really? It's pretty crowded," I replied, keeping an eye on Singh as he paced.

"Rush hour, you can't move in here," Ninel replied.

The space could easily hold thousands of people. I couldn't imagine being down here with that many people.

"Calm down, Singh," Drew said.

Singh narrowed his eyes at Drew and kept pacing. I could hear the subway train coming, its rumble shook beneath my boots. Singh turned towards the noise and watched, a small smile pulling at his lip. The train wasn't slowing down though. It wouldn't stop at this station. Singh shut his eyes, and the train flew through, inches away from him, blowing cool damp air onto the platform. Singh's hair swept back, and his coat flapped under the insult.

Ninel reached out and grabbed the back of Singh's coat and pulled him back across the line, out of the danger zone. Singh sighed, and his face fell as the train continued, the rumble getting further and further away.

I slapped his arm. "What is the matter with you?"

"I miss running. I need to get out," he complained.

"We are in a city, Singh. You can't go tearing around here," I replied.

He sighed again.

There was a low rumble. Another train was approaching at a more sedate pace. This one stopped at the platform, and the doors slid open. Most of the people who had been standing around now pressed to get on the train. It was a tight fit, like sardines in a tin can, but it seemed like everyone made it in. I lost sight of Drew and Alex, but Ninel pressed up behind me, and Singh was at my side. When the train stopped again, we funneled out, and new people clambered on. I was glad to be off, my first breath of fresh air as we climbed the steps to the street was like heaven -- If heaven was in the arctic circle. The wind had picked up, and it was snowing again. I pulled up my hood and followed along behind Vilen and Ninel to the hummer parked a few blocks over.

The heat, full blast, I rode shotgun back to Vaughn's mansion, shivering and holding my hands over the heat vents. The guys discussed the tunnels and how we could get into Metro two lines, but I ignored them. Something was gnawing at me. It wasn't Durga, but she was alert like she could feel it too. Some other force was pressing at me; a weight on my chest. I had no idea who or what it could be.

As we got out of the vehicle, Singh shifted to his lion form and swaggered into the mansion. His head was low, and I wondered if all this city living was too hard for him. Once we found Vincent, maybe we could spend time in the country.

"Any luck?" Vaughn asked from the doorway.

I shook my head, and he frowned. We both knew something was wrong, despite the assurances that Vincent was fine.

I stumbled up the stairs to the room they had given us and stripped off all the heavy outerwear. Once locked behind the bathroom door, I stripped off the rest of my layers. The hot water sprayed painfully on my skin, leaching out the cold and washing it down the drain. When I regained feeling in my hands and feet, I threw on the shorts and t-shirt I had hastily packed and abandoned the bathroom. Leaving the steam of the bathroom, I found the heat turned up in the bedroom too, but I knew the lion on the bed was even warmer. I slid under the blankets and curled up next to the purring Singh.

"I'm sorry you are unhappy," I whispered.

He rolled over and licked my cheek, scraping the skin with his harsh tongue.

"Ouch, you oaf!" I said trying to wipe his drool off on the pillow beside me.

He rested his massive head on my stomach and closed his eyes again. I fought an arm out from the blankets and pet his silly mane until he purred and I drifted off to sleep.

"Where were you before you came to me?" I asked Singh that evening as we had dinner.

"Here and there," he replied. I had convinced him to eat dinner at the table, like a person, with Vaughn and some of his vampires. I filled in Vaughn on the information we got and suggestion to check Metro two. He assured me he could get us in there, but it would take some time. The system ran the full length of the city three times over and was an underground city, of sorts. It would take a long time to search it all.

Alex made everything awkward with his strange fidgeting. He was tapping out a rhythm on his wine glass with a knife for fuck sakes. Vilen switched seats with one of Vaughn's vampires across from me and rested his massive arm across the back of Alex seat. The contact slowed the sketchy vampire.

"Will he get over this?" I asked Vilen as the rest of the table went back to the polite conversation.

"Yes, he needs time," he replied.

"I'm sorry Lark. I spent so long in those tunnels. They called me the ghost and new vampires would run from me. Some bigger vampires would chase me away.

I reached across the table and took his hand that was still twitching occasionally. Durga seized the opportunity, and I felt my hand get hot. Alex screamed and threw his other arm out, knocking dishes and glasses everywhere. He tried to pull back, but my grip was solid.

"Let go, it burns! Please!" he cried. Durga had him now and wasn't going to let go. She pulled him across the table by his arm, then clamped a hand to each side of his face. He wriggled and thrashed like a fish on the dock.

The rest of the vampires had gotten up and stood along the wall watching with horror on their faces. I was afraid she would call our knife and kill Alex, but she didn't. She used my mouth to chant in what I now recognized as Sanskrit. My hands got hotter as my arms split and multiplied. I stood, knocking my chair backwards. Singh shifted and leapt up onto the table. He stood over Alex like a menace.

The heat peaked, and Alex let out a single scream before the heat vanished and he collapsed to the table. I released him, but he lay panting and gasping for several minutes. Alex laboured breathing was the only sound in the room. Drew, of course, was the first one to speak. "Fuck," he said, righting his chair and straightening the tablecloth as much as he could with a 120 lb human and 400 lb lion holding it down. "Thank you for a wonderful meal."

"You are ... quite welcome," Vaughn said. "Could I speak to you in my study, Durga?"

Durga had curled up in her corner as soon as she destroyed dinner and did whatever she did to Alex, leaving me with the mess. Again.

"Yeah, she's not here anymore," I said, surveying the damage. "But I would be delighted to accompany you to your study."

I set up my chair and pushed it into the ruined table before turning and following Vaughn out of the room. The rest of the vampires shuffled out of my way. As we walked down the hall, the conversation began in the dining room. I wanted to smack Durga sometimes. She couldn't just be cool once! Now all these vampires would know she is a psycho too.

I followed Vaughn into his office, and he shut the door behind me. A Roar in the hall had him opening the door again to let Singh in. The lion huffed and then hopped onto the couch and collapsed. The couch groaned under his weight.

"Would you like a drink?" Vaughn asked.

"Sure," I replied. "Something strong."

Vaughn smiled and poured us each a drink. I sat in the armchair in front of his desk, and he set the glass down in front of me before walking around to take his seat.

He bit his lip for a second before he spoke. "I thought you said you and Durga worked together," he said it like he worried it would offend me.

"We do. But she is kind of dramatic sometimes and goes off."

He nodded. "Could I talk to her?"

I gave Durga a nudge, but she was not coming back. I shrugged my shoulders. "I think she can hear you. She never seems to miss an opportunity to pop in, so she must be listening."

Vaughn smiled, but it didn't reach his eyes. "I wanted to say how much I've missed her," he said with an unhappy laugh. "Others never understood, but she was perfect. She was everything. When Elliana died, I hoped she would return in her new form. When I heard Vincent found her..." He paused and looked me in the eye. "Found you, I was jealous. I thought she had chosen him, over me." He shook his head and laughed at himself.

"I was so selfish. I see now why she couldn't stay with me. There was so much to do, but I missed her. I think... I thought it was Durga that I loved, but I see you and her together now, and I know, it was Elliana that I loved back then. Maybe Durga knew all along."

Durga flashed in my eyes, and I knew what he said was true. It was still sad though.

"How did she die?" I asked. Vincent said I was immortal, and I healed so fast from even major injury, I believed him.

"I don't know. One morning she never woke up. We didn't have tests and things back then."

Durga flashed into my mind. She closed my eyes and played the memory back like I was watching an old movie on the backs of my eyelids.

Vaughn was lying in bed with Elianna. She was laughing, but there was no sound in my memory. Vaughn's eyes were bright, and his smile, wide. He said something, and she got a serious look on her face. Then she wrapped her arms around him and kissed him hard like he had just given her the most amazing news. Then Durga flashed me an image of Elianna dead in her bed, eyes half open, mouth relaxed. Vaughn shook her, and she flopped like a rag doll. Durga stood at the side of the bed. Her arms lowered with a solemn look on her face. Then she vanished and I my eyelids opened to find Vaughn right in front of me.

"What just happened?" he asked.

I bit my lip; I think it might have been his fault that Elliana died. Why would Durga show me that?

"Please?" Vaughn said.

"What did you say to her the night before she died?" I asked, already knowing the answer and dreading it too. I crossed my fingers in my lap, hoping it was inconsequential. That it was nothing.

"I asked her to marry me."

I pushed him out of the way and grabbed the trash can beside his desk, emptying my partially digested dinner into it before collapsing back into the chair.

"Whoa, are you ok?" Vaughn asked.

Singh got up and came over to purr at me. He shoved Vaughn and tried to get up in my lap in the armchair. Freaking lion.

I slid out from under his paws and ended up sitting on the floor, still nauseated and now 100% sure, I would die.

Because loving a vampire would kill me.

And I loved a vampire.

CHAPTER SIX

I went back to my room, Singh hot on my heels. The halls cleared as I walked down them and nobody looked me in the eye. I mean, Durga healed Alex. She had claimed him, and the heat meant healing, so nobody had any reason to fear her or me or us. I climbed the stairs and swung open the door to the room we were staying in.

"Thank you!" Alex said as he rushed over. Of course, he was in my room. I wanted to be alone and sulk for a few minutes, but that was too much to ask.

"Sure, no problem," I replied falling onto the bed.

Singh hopped onto the bed too and lay beside me; his furry body pressed up against my side. This was not what I was here for. I needed to stop focusing on Vincent and focus on his fallen brother. I needed to focus on what I was supposed to be doing. This was all a stupid idea.

Chasing a vampire down, professing my love to him? Dumbass.

I sat up on my bed, ignoring the incessant chattering of Alex. Crossing my legs, I placed my hands palm up on my knees. I was not a normal girl. I would not have a normal life. Time to get my shit together and stop pretending I could have any of the things I wanted.

I slowed my breathing and focused inward. Alex's voice faded away, Singh's warm back anchored me in the moment and I let my mind drift until I was numb.

* * *

I opened my eyes sitting in front of Shiva. His dreadlocked hair was whipping about like he was Medusa. His snake was slipping in and out of the wild locks as if he was a great serpent swimming through the water.

"To whom am I speaking?" Shiva asked. He had kept up this greeting since the time Durga took over my body and fooled him.

"It's Lark," I said, though I wasn't sure there was much of a gap between Durga and me anymore.

"Good day young Lark, why do you appear so dejected?"

"It doesn't matter. I wanted to talk to you about Vernon," I said.

"It matters. Is Durga a bitch again?" The Deity in question popped in waving her arms like one of those wacky inflatable waving things businesses use on street corners to get attention. She narrowed her eyes at my thought but didn't stop waving.

"I have done nothing but show Lark the way it will be if she continues on her course towards relations with the vampire." Durga scowled at me.

"Why have you done this, Durga? You have not a single romantic bone in your body," Shiva said.

"She must know what will happen. I want to keep her. She is strong and fierce and mustn't be distracted from our mission with frivolous things." "Both of you shut up," I said, standing to move around the place. It was the same temple as always. Wide arched windows with no glass allowed a breeze to pull sand through. It crunched in my teeth as I looked out across the desert. "I need to find Vernon and kill him. Then we can go somewhere else. Someplace warm at least."

I turned back to look at Shiva. He was still glaring at Durga.

"You will find happiness, Lark. Do not listen to the old hag."

"Old hag?" shrieked Durga. Her arms flapped with renewed anger.

"Yes, I'm talking about you. You can't just let her be happy?"

"You know nothing of happiness. This is the way it must be! I will not have my plans ruined because of a schoolgirl crush," Durga's voice had risen to near glass shattering level.

"It's fine. I don't care. I want to find Vernon and kill him before he ruins anything else. Vengeance for Randy and all the others Vernon has killed is what I care about." I stomped back over to where Shiva and Durga stood. "I want his blood to paint the walls. Give me his head!" My voice had risen too. My chest clenched around my strained lungs as the air heaved in and out. I focused my anger and pain, ready to do this.

Durga's smile should have set off an alarm. But at the moment I was too angry to care about Vincent. I had an outlet for my anger, and I would run with it.

"Very well, go back underground Mourning Lark. You will find your prey in the shadows," Shiva said. I ignored his frown, choosing to pretend everything was fine.

* * *

I came back to the room with Singh's head in my lap. Durga flashed behind my eyes when I blinked, and the room came back into focus. Alex sat on a chair at the end of the bed, staring at me like I had two heads. Or eight arms.

"What?" I asked.

"The prayer you say," he laughed. "It's And a Meadowlark Sang. That's the name of the prayer."

I stared at him for a moment. "That's messed up, Alex. Future reference, I don't want to know about weird shit like that, ok?" I rolled off the bed and walked towards the bathroom. As I shut the door, I realized Alex wasn't all fidgety and weird anymore. I swung it back open.

"Did Durga fix you?" I asked.

He smiled, his teeth flashing in the low light of the morning sun that streamed through the window. "She did, thank you Goddess."

I shut the door again. She didn't have to make it a huge spectacle and ruin dinner.

I took a hot shower and changed into some new clothes I purchased at the mall. Jeans and a plain t-shirt, topped with a heavy fleece hoodie, I was ready to get back to cave diving. Now was the time to find that bastard and snuff him out like a flickering flame. Then I could go home, or at least somewhere warm. My home was ruined, anyway.

I stepped back out into a flurry of activity and waving arms.

Vilen and Ninel are arguing in Russian, Drew and Singh were sitting on the bed watching, and Alex was waving his hands in the air trying to get the attention of both large vampires.

"What the hell?" I shouted. They all stopped and looked at me. "What is going on?"

"I think…" Alex started.

"He is Crazy," Vilen said.

"… I saw something in the tunnels," Alex continued.

I laughed. "I saw a lot of things in those tunnels."

"I say he is crazy," Vilen said.

"Ok, well, let's hear it anyway."

Vilen threw his hands up and turned away. Ninel's face was a mask of sorrow; frown lines etched from his lips.

"I saw a man turn into a buffalo."

Durga sprung up, turning the room red. Her rage pushed adrenaline through my system. Ninel bowed to his knee. I wasn't sure why until I realized I had my knife in my hand. Alex took a big step back, and Singh leapt off the bed and paced the room, growling and hissing.

I wanted to ask what that meant, but Durga had taken control of my mouth. Not that she was saying anything. She stood there, knife in hand, ready to fight something.

"Maybe let's take it down a notch," Drew said, breaking the tension.

Durga stormed back into her place, releasing me from her grip.

"What just happened?" I asked, setting my knife on the dresser by the wall.

"There is an old legend, Mahishasura. I say this right?" Vilen looked to Alex who just nodded.

"Durga slew him. So, the story goes." Alex sat on the corner of the bed and began his story.

"Mahishasura means Buffalo Demon. He meditated for thousands of years so he could please Lord Brahma. In return, he gained a boon. No man or God could kill him. He then waged war like no other before him. He was tyrannical and unstoppable."

"In his rage and pride, he almost destroyed the entire earth. Darkness and death covered all the land, and soon even the Gods ran away. "

"The Gods went to Brahma, Vishnu and Shiva and spoke of the troubles. They pleaded for protection or some divine intervention."

"Brahma, Vishnu and Shiva conferred for a moment before they held each other and created a beautiful light. This light was brighter than the sun. The other Gods joined in and form this light they created the Goddess Durga. She was the embodiment of Adi Shakti. As a woman, there was nothing stopping her from killing Mahishasura, for that was the loophole left behind when the arrogant man thought to become a God."

"The lords approached her, each bearing a gift that might assist her in her work."

"When each of her arms bore a weapon, she started a battle with Mahishasura. The battle raged for ten days. Mahishasura changed form to confuse Durga, but on the tenth day, she chopped off the head of the buffalo, killing Mahishasura once and for all."

"Durga restored the balance, and life returned to earth. The rivers ran clear, and the people prospered. It was Durga who saved us all, for she was just and strong."

"Shit," Drew said into the silence that followed.

"Exactly. If Mahishasura has returned, he will bring death and destruction," Alex said.

I rubbed my forehead. Durga was doing cartwheels inside me, pressing me towards the door. "Where did you see this Mahish… buffalo demon?" I asked.

"In the tunnels. There are miles of tunnels that remain unexplored, they branch off into little-known tunnels and go on for miles heading out of the city. It is an easy place to hide."

"How would we find him in the tunnels? Are we going to wander around until we stumble upon him?"

Durga lashed out. That was her plan.

"We don't have much choice," Alex said.

I threw my hands up and turned to let Durga push me out the door. The rest followed me, Singh caught up and walked pressed up against me. As I pushed out the front door, the house human scurried to hand the keys to Vilen. It was raining outside. Great.

I pulled the collar of my jacket up to my ears and hustled towards the Hummer.

"Are you going back to the tunnels?" Vaughn's voice called from behind me.

"Yup, off to find a demon," I said waving over my shoulder.

"Good luck," He called as we all climbed into the hummer. Singh decided shifting wasn't for him and stood in the foot space of the back seat as a lion. Alex, Drew and I couldn't move our legs as Singh's body pressed them into the seat, but it was better than him sitting on us.

"Is he always like this?" Alex asked, trying to move the lion forward a little.

"Yeah, pretty much," Drew replied.

The vehicle wove through the city. The streets were laid out in concentric circles around the Red Square. It looked nice on a map but meant it took a lot of time to drive a short distance. The traffic was heavy at this hour. Commuters were clashing with tourists. The city was not dull that was for sure. When I saw the tops of Saint Basil Cathedral, I knew we were getting close.

Vilen parked in the same place as last time, and we all got our waterproof clothes on. Thankfully Singh deigned to take human form for a little while. A lion on the streets of Moscow would have brought some unwanted attention. I could see it now on the 6 O'clock news; animal control trying to capture the white lion that was terrorizing the city of Moscow.

Vilen held open the drain cover, the rainwater poured down the edges, leaving a water-free area in the middle, but my chances of not getting soaked were about zero. My legs would be dry, but the rest of me was about the get cold and wet.

Ninel and Singh went down first, followed by Alex. I took a deep breath and made the plunge.

The wet steel bars were even more slippery under my boots this time, and I got both arms wet to the elbows but kept the rest of me dry by some magic, that is until I got to the bottom and had to walk through a waterfall to move away from the bottom of the ladder.

I squealed as the ice water fell over my head and down my neck. Shit, my life sucked. I would kill this buffalo guy slowly for making me come down here to get him. Vernon would die painfully too for bringing me to this stupid city.

And Vincent… well, I wouldn't think about Vincent, wherever he was. Ok, that was wishful thinking. He was always on my mind. Even when I should think about where I'm putting my feet, I was thinking about stupid Vincent. That's why when I stepped on something sticking out of the water, I tripped and ended up on hands and knees in the gross swamp water.

Something squished between my fingers and the dirty water soaked into my sleeves.

"Well, fuck," I muttered as I rose from the filth.

I heard a stifled laugh. I knew exactly who it was too. That little shit, Drew. I turned slowly to look at him. Durga helped by turning my eyes red, so when I locked on him, he took a step back and lost all humour.

"I'm sorry, Durga," he muttered.

"You will be," I replied.

We carried on through the tunnels, climbing up and down from one system to the next until we arrived at the center of the Red Square. It was a cavernous space of smooth cement. The ceiling was low, but it was wide, and the water coming through the drains ran away with some speed, unlike the lazy water in other tunnels. Rivers rushed beneath our feet, weaving around our boots. Above, the dim light of day came through the grates. It darkened anytime a pedestrian hustled over, then flicked back on, like a switch. It was eerie to be right beneath all those people. They didn't know we were down there.

We marched on heading south, following the flow of the water. My breath hung in the air, and my wet skin started to tingle with the numbing cold.

We came out of the smooth tunnel into a wide brick tunnel. Alex stopped at the mouth of this tunnel.

"Watch your step. The Neglinnaya river is deeper. You might not want to go for a swim." He smiled and then moved along the edge where there was a walkway. The water was dark and moved at a reasonable pace.

The tunnel curved up ahead. I could hear traffic above, and the occasional honk echoed through the underground.

"You know some people come down here just to explore," Alex said, disrupting the sound of our feet on the brick walkway.

"I can see why," I said. It was a magical world. Like a different planet. The echoes and the rushing water. The way it muffled the city sounds; it was peaceful. If it was warmer, I might say it was fun to climb around down here.

We scuttled along beside the Neglinnaya River for several more minutes before we heard voices up ahead.

"Watch your step; the brick is crumbling here. Please stay close to the wall."

As we came around the next bend, we were face to face with a group of people with cameras led by a bored looking vampire in hip waders. I looked back, thankful that Singh had returned to human form.

"David," Alex said in a tone that indicated he didn't like this David person.

"Alex, you starting your own tour guide business?" David laughed.

"No, this is Lark."

David's eyes landed on me and grew round, but he said nothing, he just stared at me.

"Where is the king?" David whispered low enough the humans behind him wouldn't hear. I still hadn't thought much about that part of the prophecy that Alex had been spittering when we first met him.

"He is lost," Alex replied.

David's eyes grew wide. He turned to his group of tourists. "Everyone please, move against the wall and let these diggers pass."

There was muttering about diggers and excited smiles as we walked by. Diggers were what Moscow's tunnel explorers called themselves. It was a cult almost, Alex had explained to me. Vampires and humans who came down here day after day to find new tunnels and map them.

Once we were past the tourists, I felt Durga shove me hard. I took off, my feet slapping against the brick walkway in my clumsy rubber boots.

Let's go!" Drew yelled behind me. The sound of them chasing, pushed me to go faster. I rounded another corner and slammed to a stop in front of a small drain that was running water down into the Neglinnaya. I scrambled up into it and stood. It was just tall enough for me to stand, the guys would have to crawl. I didn't wait for them though. I took off at a sprint and nearly collided with my target as I came around a corner.

My knife flashed into my hand, and the vampire dropped the human in the water at his feet. He hissed at me and launched himself towards me, his disgusting nails aimed for my throat.

I ducked forward and slammed my knife into his stomach, but that didn't slow him down. His teeth snapped together as he tried to get them into my neck. I pulled my knife out of his stomach and got my foot between us as he knocked me to the ground. His weight pressed down, but Durga gave me enough strength to kick him off me. I rose and tried to get the upper hand, but he launched himself off the far wall and slammed into me again, knocking my head off the brick wall. Durga screamed and slashed at him several times as his teeth edged closer and closer to my throat before she got in the killing blow and the vampire collapsed onto of me. I was dizzy for a moment so rested there with the putrid vampire still on top of me.

"Oh shit," I heard a lot of splashing, and then someone ripped the weight off, and Drew's concerned face looked down at me.

I gave him a little wave, and he shook his head.

"You scared the shit out of me," he said, offering me his hand. I took it and let him pull me up out of the slime and water. It had drenched through. No waterproof pants could hold up to that insult.

The rest of the guys came crawling in. Alex could stand, but he had to hunch over, he couldn't see where he was going and almost collided with Ninel when he stopped moving.

"I guess you found a bad one," Alex said, sheathing a knife into his boot. Good to know he came armed.

"Yeah, he drained that poor guy." They all looked at the man in the hip waders and helmet. He looked like the people on the tour of the underground we had passed. That would not be good for business.

CHAPTER SEVEN

We slogged through the tunnels and out to the street. Even with Vilen's coat thrown over my shoulders and wrapped around me, violent shivers racked my body. I would need way better waterproof clothes if I was going to wrestle the occasional bad guy in the tunnels.

I had a hot shower and moseyed down to the kitchen. Inside a few vampires were cooking up a storm.

I tried to walk to the fridge to have a peek for a snack, but a pretty Burnette vampire caught me. Her hair sat on top of her head in a bun, and her dark eyes glittered in the bright lights of the industrial-sized kitchen. She was a vampire, but her features were delicate like she belonged in a china cabinet.

"I can make you something!" She said. "A sandwich. Some soup. A souffle?"

I laughed. "Uhm, I was just going to fix something for myself, you don't have to go to the bother."

"Oh, I don't mind at all! You don't remember me, do you?"

I took another look at the vampire. She didn't ring any bells.

"That's ok! You had a lot going on. I was living in Canada, with Ajax. Before, you know..."

"Shit, I'm sorry. I still feel bad about getting you guys blown up."

"It's fine. I came here for a visit while they rebuilt our home and decided I liked it here so much, I didn't want to leave. So, here I am!" She waved her arms around the kitchen like a game show host. Weird, but at least she wasn't afraid of me.

She grabbed things out of the fridge and cut fresh bread. When she finished, she handed me a beautiful sandwich with some fresh veggies on the side.

"Thank you," I said, my mouth watering.

She pulled out a chair and waved me to sit down.

I sat and took a bite of my sandwich. It was freaking delicious.

"What's your name?" I asked around the next mouthful of food like I was born in a barn and had no manners.

She smiled. "Kelly."

"Nice to meet you, Kelly. I'm Lark," I replied taking another big bite of the sandwich. The crunchy lettuce and the thinly sliced ham brought a hum to my lips.

"I know who you are," she laughed. Of course, she did, every vampire knew of me by now. Durga did a little happy flip inside me. She wanted everyone to fear me, to fear us.

When I finished my lunch, I thanked Kelly and went out to find Vaughn. I knocked on his office door, but he wasn't there, so I wandered the house until I bumped into the house human.

"Hey, have you seen Vaughn?" I asked.

The human spun on his heel to face me. "Oh, yes. He is in his room."

"Ok, where is his room?" I asked. The man bit his lip like he wasn't sure he should tell me.

"It's on the third floor. First door on your right."

"Thank you," I replied — odd human.

I climbed the stairs and knocked on the door.

"Come in," I heard Vaughn say from beyond the door.

I opened it to find him laying on the bed in a robe shuffling through pages.

"Oh. Hi Lark," he said sitting up and putting his pages aside. "I thought you were someone else."

"I'm sorry, I can talk to you later," I said, closing the door.

"No, it's fine. Come in."

It was awkward talking to him when he was undressed.

"I was going to update you. We didn't get very far before we ran into a fallen vampire. I took care of him. I thought you should know."

"Thank you. One of my vampires reported seeing Vernon in the Red Square today."

"Shit, we were close to him. I need to get back out there. I don't know how he is hiding from me."

There was a knock at the door just before it swung open to reveal a tall, slim woman who looked like a model. She was wearing a short trench coat, and high heels and I imagined not much else.

She smiled at me and then said something in Russian to Vaughn. His face went pink, and he shook his head. I looked back at the woman, then back to Vaughn.

"I'll…talk to you later, Vaughn."

He said nothing as I scurried out the door.

I did not want to know.

I gathered the team, and we hit an outdoor supply store on our way back to the tunnels.

Decked out in a waterproof outfit, the sales clerk guaranteed to keep me dry in the tunnels, I stepped down the steel ladder and into the darkness.

This time we wandered the tunnels heading north. Leaving the beaten paths, we walking for hours. Our new headlamps did a wonderful job of lighting the tunnels, showing the old bricks and stalactites. We were like proper diggers now, but we weren't here for exploration. We were hunting. I sent out my senses a few times, but apart from the occasional vampire that seemed to be above us, I didn't pick up anything.

The dampness and cold were getting to me, and it was getting late, but I sent out my senses one last time expecting to feel nothing when I felt a tug. Durga pulled my senses back in and pushed my feet into a run. I was clunky running in a full waterproof get up but tore through the tunnels. Water splashed and echoed through the tunnel until it opened into a mining cave. There were rail tracks on the ground and up ahead, and the water dried until we were running over rotting wooden railway sleepers between the tracks. We rounded the next corner to find the tunnel widened before it narrowed again into a small boarded up cave opening. Someone had ripped one board down, so there was enough space for a person to get through. I slid to a stop and climbed between the boards when I saw dozens of glowing red eyes. Arms reached out for me as one latched on from behind, ripping me back through the opening. I didn't have time to thank Ninel though as a horde of fallen vampires flooded out of the cave, breaking the remaining boards.

My knife flashed into my hands, and my vision turned crimson. Durga was keen to play. The vampires were on us in a second. I slashed and stabbed at them. One got a hold of my right arm and clamped its filthy teeth down, puncturing my brand-new waterproof coat and flesh beneath. I switched my knife to my left hand and stabbed the vampire in the top of his head. When he reared back, I stabbed him in the throat and his blood mixed with mine to run down my arm. He collapsed to the ground. I felt no pain, but the blood on my right hand made my grip slippery. The sounds of battle and death filled the tunnels. My heart raced in my chest, pushing me to move faster and fight harder. As I plunged my knife toward the next vampire, my grip slipped. I had never dropped my knife before, but when it hit the ground, the horde of vampires took me down, slamming my head off the steel railway track. The yells and screams from the team faded for a minute as the sharp ringing in my skull dazed me. As soon as my mind cleared, Durga blasted forward, dividing my arms and multiplying them until I was in a sea of vampires and fighting them with all of my weapons at once. Singh had pressed his way to the front, and Durga pulled my lips into a smile as she watched him tear the head off a vampire. Our arms swung with grace as we stood with the poise of centuries of battles, slaying decrepit vampire after vampire. When silence fell, and we had vanquished our quarry, she receded but not before she looked to Ninel and smiled.

Ninel was still smiling as my vision returned to normal. A river of red ran at our feet along with a sea of bodies. Blood stained Singh's white coat, matching the walls. The lion purred as he licked his talons, sitting in a puddle of blood.

"Well, that was fun," Alex said as he sheathed his knife and tried to wipe the blood from his face, smearing it around like war paint.

We picked our way back out of the tunnel, stepping over the fallen vampires we had slaughtered. I had never seen so many in one place before. Rogues grouped up, but the fallen seemed to be solitary. I glanced back at the small tunnel they had come from.

"Are you thinking, what I'm thinking?" Drew asked.

I stopped walking and tried to see past the ruined wood that was still partially blocking the small tunnel.

"You think they were guarding something?" I asked.

Drew shrugged his shoulders. The rest of the team noticed we stopped and came back to join the discussion.

"Is old mine shaft. Could be very long," Vilen said.

"We're here now, might as well look," I said.

I worked my way back through the vampire bodies and stepped through the wider hole they made in the wood that had blocked the entrance to the old shaft. The ceiling was low. I had to stoop, the guys had to crawl, and it was not a smooth floor. The uneven ground was rough between the rail tracks. After an hour of slow progress, the ceiling opened, but it came to a dead end.

"Complete waste of time." I kicked a rock, frustrated. I needed a break from this crap. We turned around and picked our way back out of the mine shaft.

When we approached the entrance of the tunnel, Ninel, who had been leading the way, froze, staring out the broken doorway.

"What is it?" I asked pressing past Vilen's broad back to peek around Ninel's shoulder.

All the bodies of the fallen vampires had vanished.

"Oh, shit." Drew voiced it perfectly.

CHAPTER EIGHT

The whole walk back I couldn't stop thinking about the disappearing bodies. Something weird was going on in these tunnels. There were at least thirty dead vampires. All of them removed while we were down that mine shaft without a trace. I wanted to turn around, go back and look again, like I had missed something. We went over the area before we left though. There was nothing there. They had vanished. It was a damn mystery.

At the Hummer, we stripped out of our waterproof suits. We rinsed off most of the blood by wading into the Neglinnaya river before we exited. Each of the outfits came with a patch kit, so Vilen said he would patch up the arm of my suit where the vampire had torn it.

I was silent on the way back to Vaughn's mansion. The strange experience in the tunnel played over in my mind.

We went back down into the tunnels the next day. As we rounded a corner the sound of music reverberated through the tunnel. I followed it until we came upon a large space filled with vampires. Like the first large group we found, there were some humans in the mix, Unlike the first group, this one was accompanied by the scent of blood hanging in the air.

"What the hell?" I whispered from the doorway to the square room. It looked like a theater, the ground sloped downward and the vampires danced and lurched around each other.

"Let's go a different way," Ninel said in my ear.

Durga rose up and flashed my eyes to red. The scent of blood was strong enough that Durga was not going to leave without an explanation.

She shoved me forward into the writhing crowd. Vampires on all sides stopped dancing and backed away as I marched through. The further I walked into the space, the stronger the scent was.

"Durga," I heard whispered over and over. I was pretty obvious with my red eyes, but Durga's rage increased as we moved forward and my arms split, producing weapons.

A vampire screamed and tried to run away, but my muscle had barricaded the entrance.

Vampires cowered and the music stopped abruptly.

"Please, Durga, we don't kill anyone!" a vampire cried out from the front.

Durga pushed me in the direction of the voice. What I found at the front was the biggest shock of my life.

There were dozens of humans, with knives in their hands and small cuts on their nearly naked bodies. Their eyes were lidded, like they were drunk or high. I stopped walking and watched as one slid the knife across his arm and offered it to a vampire that was standing behind him as if he was oblivious to the fact all the vampires were staring at me.

"What is going on here?" Durga's voice echoed through the now silent room. No answer was forthcoming so she moved me forward towards a human. "What are you doing?" she asked a woman dressed in only a sports bra and shorts. Her arms had several shallow cuts and there was one on her thigh that was weeping.

"I'm feeding them," she said in a dreamy voice.

Durga retreated, satisfied that the human was here of her own will. This, of course, left me with the mess she created here.

I scratched my neck and turned to face the room full of frightened vampires. When they saw my eyes had returned to normal, they relaxed.

"Alright, uhm, sorry to interrupt. Carry on," I said as I made my way back to the entrance where the team was waiting.

Oops.

The next two weeks went by. We found no more fallen vampires. Even though we went back to the start of the mine shaft several times, it was always empty and looked untouched. Durga was always pushing me towards the door, determined to find the bloody buffalo demon, but I had long since lost my interest in everything to do with Moscow. That is how I found myself in a bar at three AM.

"One more," I called to the bartender who had looked ready to cut me off after my last drink. He brought me another but admonished me in Russian. His face a mask of disapproval. I didn't speak Russian, so I didn't feel the slightest bit chastised.

I sipped my drink and stared at myself in the mirror that lined the wall behind the liquor bottles. Right in front of me, there was a bottle missing, leaving a gap so I could see my reflection. I had pulled my straight dark hair up into a ponytail several hours ago; before our most recent stomp through the dank tunnels. Wisps of hair had escaped the elastic, making me look like I had been through a hurricane. With no makeup on, my pale features were even starker. The alcohol didn't add colour to my cheeks like most people. I wished my skin was more olive like my mothers had been. I got her hair; I remembered that much about her. She had the same dark straight hair that slid over her shoulders. She would hold it back with one hand when she reached into the oven to get out dinner or when she bent over to pick up the toys I had left on the floor. Her hair. What a silly thing to remember.

I downed the last of my drink and turned away from the mirror. The stool beside me was empty, and I wished that Frankie was there. His magic had limits. I knew thinking about him wouldn't bring him here, but I thought about him and wished, anyway. Taking out my phone, I read over his last text messages. I typed him a new message, but deleted it and put my phone away. Drunk texts would be regrets in the morning. Maybe I wasn't drunk enough yet.

"Are you ready to go home yet?" Ninel asked from the barstool on the other side of me.

"No, unless by home, you mean America." I snorted a laugh. "I don't have a home there anymore either. So, I guess this bar is my home now."

"We close in one hour," The Russian man behind the bar said. I guess he spoke English after all.

"You hear that, Ninel? In one hour, I will be homeless. Maybe I'll make the sewers my home. I can curl up with the giant mythical rat at night."

"That is not a myth," Alex said sliding onto Frankie's stool. I scowled at him, but he didn't seem to notice.

"It is a myth," the bartender said.

"I have seen it!" Alex protested. He was loud. His voice rang in my ears, and I gave him a shove.

"Move down one seat!" I said. He looked at me for a moment and then slid over. Frankie's seat was once again vacant. That didn't last though. The other annoying man in my life, Singh plopped down on the bar stool, rested an elbow on the bar and his head in his hand, so he was looking at me.

"What?" I asked.

"Is this the new improved Lark?" He asked.

"Who said I needed improving? I was happier before all this crap came into my life."

"Were you?" he asked, a mocking look of disbelief on his face.

"Shut up," I said, turning back to my mirror. "And get out of Frankie's seat."

I looked the same. My head was heavy, so I let it fall forward to the bar a little too hard. The impact sent a ring through my ears, but I was numb enough it didn't hurt. I lifted my head and let it fall a few more times on the hard, brass bar.

I wanted to go home but I couldn't. At least not until I found this buffalo and Vernon and killed them and then hunted down Vincent to make sure he was ok. He could be dead, for all I knew; Despite Vaughn's assurances.

"Come on, Kitten. Time for bed," Singh said, sliding my arm around his shoulders. There was no way I could walk like that, he was too tall, but when Ninel wrapped my other arm over his shoulders, and the two of them stood up, they suspended me off the ground like a hammock between two trees. They walked a few paces before I yelled at them to put me down. They did, because, in this day and age, they are likely to get their asses kicked by the bouncers if they didn't, but Singh kept his arm around me, ushering me to the door. The night air was bitter. The wind whipped down the street and blew rain in my face. It was early spring, but mother nature didn't seem to know that. Some tulips had sprouted in the gardens around the city. They were hardier than I was. I watched the ones outside the bar sway in the breeze. Their lush green leaves were whipping about. The flower heads were still closed tight, waiting for their perfect moment to bloom and show the world they had beaten the odds and survived beneath frozen soil all winter. They mocked me with their strength and determination.

"Stop scowling at the vegetation and get in the damn vehicle," Singh said.

I scowled at him, then got in the damn vehicle. Since when was Singh the voice of reason. I thought he had settled on the being the one who voted for naps. Maybe my binge drinking was cutting into his nap time.

That thought proved correct when I collapsed on my bed, and a white lion collapsed beside me. Within minutes he was snoring away, hogging all the blankets. I had long since learned not to bother fighting with the big jerk. I curled around him and let my eyes drift closed.

When my eyes opened again, the sun was streaming through the open window blinds. I rolled over and hid my head under the pillow, realizing only a moment later that I was alone in the room. I hadn't been alone in a room, or a bed in weeks. Stretched out like a starfish, I occupied all the bed. I pulled the blankets up over my head, and they came untucked from the bottom with a quick tug, so I was in a peaceful dim fort. No more sun searing my retinas and the heat of my cocoon was delicious.

My phone made a blip, alerting me to a text message. I snuck one arm out of my cocoon and fumbled around on the bedside table until my fingers found the cell phone and then pulled it back into my secret oasis. The light from the screen was almost as bright as the sun, but I squinted at it with one eye and read the bleary text. It was from Frankie.

"I miss you, hope you will be home soon," he wrote.

I wanted to say I missed him too, but Durga's warning had left me cautious of what I was doing and saying. Dying for a guy was stupid.

I typed a reply and then deleted it. As I was about to put the phone down, Durga took over and sent Frankie a text. I watched as the words appeared on the small screen and tried to stop her before she hit send, but it was too late. Holy fuck! "Holy fuck!" I repeated out loud as Durga slid back into her place inside me, pleased as punch.

"I want that too," Frankie replied. Durga had no chill. Now Frankie thought I wanted way more from him than I ever imagined and he wanted that too. No more text privileges for Durga. I might as well drunk-text with her around. I popped my arm out of the blanket and threw my phone across the room.

"Ouch. what the hell?"

I popped the blanket down to see who I had hit. It was only Drew, so I pulled the blanket back up and curled up in my fort. My super blanket fort of invisibility.

"Are you still drunk?" he asked.

"Maybe," I muttered. It would be better if I were. But it was possible I was losing my mind and just didn't care anymore.

"Maybe we need a day off, you know today is the Victory Day Parade. Why don't we spend the day *on* the streets instead of under them?"

I peeked out from the corner of the blanket. That might be fun.

"Come on, get yourself cleaned up, it smells like a bar in here."

I threw a pillow at him, and he squealed before dashing out of the room and closing the door behind him. After worming my way out from under the blankets, I staggered to the washroom. As the shower warmed up, steam billowed over the curtain, and I turned to look at myself in the mirror. I looked drunk still, but the start of a hangover headache was coming on. I rifled through the cabinets until I found pain relievers and popped a couple.

Durga wouldn’t heal my hangover unless necessary for vampire killing, so I would suffer unless I took something. I swallowed the pills down with a few glasses of water for good measure. My shower was quick. With no interest in drying my hair today, I tied it up wet. I could wear my hat. It was sunny out, and the warm weather had arrived. It wasn’t hot, but it wasn’t arctic anymore either.

I walked back out of the washroom, feeling about fifty percent better. Singh was in my room as a human for once. He only shifted if we were in town, but the house was a lion friendly zone.

“What’s up?” I asked.

"I’m coming to the parade." He smiled at me, and his canines were still long and pointed like a lion. "I haven’t been to a parade in a long time."

“Singh, you have a little something,” I said pointing to my teeth.

He reached up to his mouth and felt his teeth, then hissed at me. “How about now?”

I laughed and threw a sock at him. He growled and chucked it back. We moseyed down the stairs giggling like idiots. It felt good.

I followed him into the dining room. The smell of bacon turned my stomach, but I choked some down. I would not turn my nose up at bacon, no matter how much rum I drank the night before. It seemed to help settle my stomach anyway, and a couple of glasses of orange juice cleared my head. When we walked out the door, I felt better than I had in a while. Alex stayed behind. He said he had seen too many Victory Day parades and would rather gnaw off his hand than see another. So, Vilen and Ninel came with Drew and Singh and I. We headed out to see the sights.

"We should take metro," Vilen said. His Russian accent seemed thicker today. As if the patriotic day made him more Russian. "Will be no space for parking."

"OK, lead the way," I said.

We followed Vilen's broad back through the gates and out onto the sidewalk. It was a few blocks before we came to the first entrance to the subway. It was a small building with pillars in front. I dreaded going back underground, but as we climbed down the stairs, I realized it was spacious with archways and wide platforms. There were only a few other people waiting for the train. We must be closer to the start of the metro line. We stepped onto the train when it pulled up, and I sat down on a seat beside Singh.

"So, what is this Victory Day about, anyway?" I asked him, popping gum into my mouth.

"It marks the end of World War two," Singh explained. "It's overblown here in Moscow. The people have a lot of pride and make it a big show."

He took the gum from my hand. I only got it out for him, he had eaten steak raw for breakfast, and his breath smelled like pennies. I made the mistake of telling him his breath smelled once. I would not do that again. Cats hold grudges and waking up with his butt in my face was not fun.

More and more people kept getting on the train until I wasn't comfortable sitting anymore. Feeling claustrophobic was crazy after all the time I had spent in the tunnels, but people standing over me had a different effect. A nice older lady took my seat when I offered it, and I took her place at a pole, jammed between Ninel and a stranger. By the time we got off the subway, people had packed into the train, and we spilled out on to the platform. The platform here was ornate and beautiful. It ran between two sets of tracks, with a high ceiling and attractive circular cut outs that were so well lit, it felt like being in a mall instead of underground. Once we had gathered ourselves, we climbed the stairs to the rising sounds of music and feet marching on stone. We exited a beautiful building at the top of the stairs, its design fit the theme of the old buildings in the city.

The crowds were everywhere. I wasn't sure how many people were in Moscow, but I was sure they were all in the streets. The sun blared down on us, warming my skin through my jacket. And the percussion of drums beat in my chest through the loudspeakers. Singh slung an arm over my shoulders and guided me through the crowd till we made it to the front and could see the Red Square.

Soldiers in bright red uniforms marched in exaggerated steps, carrying flags. Hundreds more stood in perfect rows in front of the Kremlin. Tanks rolled in, and soldiers moved along beside the heavy artillery in formation. They marched in such perfect time that their feet shook the ground.

Overhead, planes flew in formation too. Their coloured tails tracked through the sky long after they went by, making the whole city feel like a magical land. A marching band played, and the surrounding people cheered. The Red Square filled with marching soldiers; their white gloves swung in unison as they marched. It made them seem like they were more machines than men and the musicians moved in perfect synchronization.

Soldiers of all varieties turned to look at one place and saluted. I peeked out in front of Singh and realized the president was standing on a podium and all the men and women were saluting him as they passed. Behind me, people shouted, and children cheered. I turned around to see the crowd. They all had flags and banners or blown up photos of soldiers.

It was overwhelming. Scattering my senses but the joy pulled a smile to my face. This was a special day for everyone here, and you could feel the pride of the people. I let my eyes trail over the crowd of people, taking in the children's faces and the old men dressed in uniform watching the young men march to the beat they must have once marched to.

A familiar face jumped out of the crowd. I focused in and red eyes locked with mine. A smile curved the cruel mouth before it disappeared in the sea of people.

I pushed Singh's arm off me and pressed through the crowd. The people made way, but not fast enough.

"Move people!" I yelled. Singh was hot on my heels. The people were packed so tight that many of them couldn't move, but Durga pressed me to run. I couldn't run. Fuck.

I pushed through to the back of the crowd and looked up and down the street. He was gone.

"Who was it?" Singh asked form right behind me.

"Vernon," I replied. "He's here all right."

"Let's split up," Drew said.

"No one should go alone," Ninel suggested.

I strode off down the street heading North. He couldn't have gotten too far. I stopped. If he was nearby, I could track him. I took a deep calming breath and sent out my senses.

My senses flooded out like an overflowing coffee cup to coat the city. At first, I found nothing: a few vampires sitting around, but no Vernon. Then I noticed something I hadn't before. There was a blank space where my senses flowed over and around, but not through. It was in the tunnels. I had felt nothing like that before. It was as if a small part of the city didn't even exist.

"Get the rest of the guys. We need to go in the tunnels," I said.

Ninel took out his phone and made a call.

This was just the break I needed.

Finally.

CHAPTER NINE

We took the metro past the crush of the parade and met up with another vampire who had brought our hummer, waterproof clothes, and Alex. Changing in a different back alley this time, we suited up in a hurry. Durga rushed me and was shouting commands.

"I will not wait for you, vampires," she spit. I tried to hush her, but she was a woman scorned and would not calm down.

Alex was jittery. Not the way he was when we pulled him out of the tunnels but amped up.

Drew pulled his headlamp on, and Durga herded the team to the closest culvert.

We landed in a different tunnel this time, but it was newer, smooth cement instead of old brick. This tunnel led to a drop off into the Neglinnaya River. We had to wade through the river and climb back up onto the walkway on the far side. It was higher than my waist and had the current pressed on me like a stiff breeze. It was colder in the tunnels than on the streets now. Summer was on its way.

"Let me check and see which way we should go," I said. I closed my eyes and sent out my senses. There were a few more vampires in the Red Square, but I searched out from there until I felt that blank space again. It was eerie like an abandoned house. It made the hair on my arms stand on end.

I shivered as my senses came back to my body. I pointed north, and we shuffled along the brick walkway towards the darkness.

Stopping twice more, I narrowed it down to the area near where we met the fallen vampires, but it wasn't down that tunnel. We had searched there. It was adjacent to the tunnel, somehow.

We circled back several times trying different routes. Even Alex didn't know where we were trying to go. I half thought about letting Durga bash through the wall, but destabilizing the old walls didn't sound like a brilliant plan.

"There must be a way to get in," I said, sliding down to sit on a pile of old rail ties stacked by the wall.

"I am telling you, there is nothing over there," Alex moaned again.

"And I am telling you, there is something. It's dark and creepy and trying to hide from me!"

Alex dropped his eyes to the ground. Drew bit his lip like he didn't want to argue with me, but hours ago I felt like he had given up finding this place I was talking about. He didn't believe me either.

"We will find it," Ninel said. He believed me, at least.

I pulled out my bottled water and down the dribble at the bottom. It was the last we had brought down with us. Chances were good we would have to abandon this search and come back again. I tipped my head back against the wall and closed my eyes. A heavy sigh racked my lungs.

Singh's purr was the only warning before his furry face rubbed across mine. His mane got in my mouth, and I spent the next several minutes trying to pick fluff off my tongue, but I appreciated his support. With a sigh, I stood up and followed the team back down the tunnel.

Just before we turned back south on the Neglinnaya, I noticed a smaller tunnel up high on the wall near the ceiling. A slow trickle of water ran out of it and traced a path down the wall leaving a trail of hard water, but someone disturbed the trail, like someone had climbed the wall.

I didn't follow the team. Instead, I looked at the markings and tried to figure out how someone could have climbed it. A human couldn't, but a vampire could. I reached up to get a handle on the wall, but it was too smooth.

"You want a boost?" Ninel asked from behind me. He cupped his hands, and I stepped up into them before he heaved me up into the narrow entrance. I could only crawl once inside. Singh's huff let me know he was behind me and I heard more quiet rustles as the rest of the team climbed in to follow me.

I couldn't see the end of the tunnel, but at one point ahead there was daylight streaming down and flickering off and on like people were walking over it. We must be closer to the street as the drain had a slight rise to it and the sounds of the roads were getting louder.

When I was under the grate, I realized it wasn't people walking over it. We were under the busy road that circled the Red Square. The traffic was heavy. No one would attempt to use this as an entry to the tunnels. I moved just past the culvert and my eyes adjusted to the dark as my headlamp caught on the end of the tunnel. There was an opening another hundred feet along that seemed to lead to another section of sewers. Before I moved on, I sent my senses forward, but that darkness was all around me. I couldn't sense anything ahead or behind me. Like a dark hole had swallowed me up and the rest of the world had disappeared.

"We are inside," I whispered into the dark. Singh let out a tiny huff, and I moved forward.

The tension was thick. Everyone whispered through the tunnel. Durga was anxious, turning in my stomach. I felt her wanting to push forward and have me rush the last section of the drain, but she held off. Crawling forward, a piece of glass I hadn't noticed in the now dry tunnel stuck in my hand. I hissed and pulled the glass out, but blood pooled in the palm. I let the skin seal up before moving forward again, Leaving a trail of blood on the dirty cement.

As I approached the opening, Singh used his massive paw to flatten me to the ground and slid over me so he could go first. Stupid lion. He stepped on my hair, pulling several strands out as he stumbled on. I couldn't even swear at him as we were all in silent mode.

He disappeared over the edge of the tunnel to space below on silent feet. I swung around and slid over the edge too, losing sight of the space as my headlamp fell off and crashed to the ground. Standing in the dark, my heart raced with uncertainty before my eyes adjusted and the reality of the situation struck home.

I had hoped to find Vernon, but what I found instead sent ice through my veins.

There, nailed to the wall, like Jesus to the cross, was Vincent. And he wasn't moving.

CHAPTER TEN

I slammed my light back on my head and rushed forward. Thick steel nails suspended Vincent, driven through his wrists and ankles. They pinned him to the cement wall behind him. His clothes, torn and singed like he had been through an explosion. His head hung limp to one side, his eyes closed.

I reached out towards him, but there was some kind of invisible wall in front of him.

Singh took a swing at it with his claws, but they slid off the invisible wall too.

My knife flashed into my hand. I stabbed at the invisible wall and tried to pry my knife into the cement at the edge, but it was too strong.

The rest of the team landed in the cavernous room.

"Oh shit. What the hell?" Drew said.

He walked forward and tried to reach out to the nail holding one of Vincent's arms to the wall, but hit the force field too.

Vilen pounded on the center of the force field. It sounded like his fist was hitting a metal drum, reminding me of the battle at Frankie's warehouse, when the witches were protecting each other with force fields.

I unzipped my jacket and had to take my waterproof gear all of, but fished out my phone and tried to send a text to Frankie.

The message failed to send.

"I have to go back to the culvert," I said.

"Who are you calling?" Alex asked.

"My friend Frankie, He knows magic, and this is magic," I replied as Vilen gave me a boost and a concerned look.

"You are friends with warlocks and witches?" Vilen asked.

"Yeah, well, one of them anyway," I said before sliding through the tunnel back to the access point at the busy street. Hopefully, I would have reception there.

I lay in the tunnel under the street as cars flashed a strobe light above me and hit send again.

This time it went through.

A moment later my phone rang an incoming call. I had expected a text, so the ringtone startled me.

"Hello?"

"What are you doing?" he asked.

"I found Vincent. He's behind a force field though. Like the one you used."

"Shit," he said. "I should have come with you." He sighed and repeated shit a few more times.

"Can you tell me how you make it? Durga has magic, right? She might take it down."

Durga rolled in my stomach. I had felt her frustration at first, but now she was on team Lark. The magic people knew magic, and that was what we needed.

"The force field is like firmness if that makes sense. You have to be rigid and sharp to make it, and the same feeling takes it down."

It made little sense, but Durga flashed on the backs of my eyelids, holding a thunderbolt in her hand. If she had a plan, I'd go with that.

"Ok, Durga has a plan. I'll let you go; I don't have service down here."

"Where are you?"

"Under the city, in the tunnels."

"Be careful Lark. Come home soon."

"I will," I said.

I hung up and slid the phone back into my pocket before securing myself back into my waterproof suit. I rolled over and pushed up on all fours. After a few failed attempts at getting turned around in the tight space, I crawled backwards to the drop-off. I flopped back into the cavern with a thud. When I stood up and turned around, Durga took over. My headlight shone red as she looked through my eyes and the guys backed away from Vincent. She doubled my arms and then doubled them again until I stood in her image. A replica of the Goddess she once was and armed with weapons gifted to her form the Gods themselves. My arms waved like branches in a stiff breeze until the arm holding the lightning bolt came to the front.

I could feel the magic in the room swell and the vampires each took another step back. Singh came next to me and pressed into my side. His warmth wrapped around me, feeding my will and determination.

The magic of the lightning bolt sizzled on my palm. It arched across the space, lighting the room in a marvel of colour. Durga pointed the bolt of lightning at Vincent. The force field around him turned to ash and rained to the floor with a clap that echoed through the tunnel system.

Durga stepped forward. She stared at Vincent for a moment before she reached forward and touched his face. I had a moment of shock as she cupped his cheek. I felt her affection for him and desire. It didn't make sense that she would warn me away from him, but before I could think any further, Vincent's muscles bunched and he flung himself forward, pulling the steel nails from the wall with a yell. Durga jumped backwards. Vincent pulled the steel from his feet, letting each one clash on the floor. Then he pulled them from his hands. His eyes flashed red, and his teeth lengthened. He held the steel stakes as weapons.

Durga waved her arms, her weapons at the ready too. I pushed at Durga, trying to regain control. Killing Vincent would kill me. I couldn't do it. Durga paused for a moment, just long enough for Vincent to throw both stakes at me. They embedded deep in my stomach and knocked me over backwards. Shouting followed, but it seemed distant as I lay on the cement floor staring into the darkness above, gasping for breath. Tipping my head down, I tried to look at my stomach but it was too dark, my headlamp must have fallen off. There was more yelling, but it was quieter now, distant. The smell of blood reached my nose and then it was all I could smell and taste. I coughed and a viscous fluid sprayed out of my mouth, raining back down on me like I was a sick fountain. I closed my eyes for a second.

"Lark."

I opened my eyes, but something filtered the voice like I was listening from under water. My vision wavered. Drew came into focus for a moment, his face hovering over me and a bright halo above his head. I smiled and tried to reach out to him, but my arms weren't working.

"Lark, hang on, ok?" Drew said. He was so pretty. Then his halo went out, and I was alone in the darkness.

CHAPTER ELEVEN

My eyes opened, and I was in the room Vaughn had set me up in. I closed my eyes again but had a flash of yelling and blood and darkness and sat straight up in bed. My heart pounded in my chest, I looked down, but there was no blood.

A massive paw knocked me back down on the bed and a cold lion nose bopped my cheek before an epic purr started that sounded more like a motorboat.

"What happened?" I asked the lion, but Singh didn't shift back. Luckily, there was someone else in the room.

"The guys dragged you back here with two metal rail spikes in your stomach." Kelly stood at the end of my bed. "I got you cleaned up and changed you. The rest of your team is downstairs, but your silly cat wouldn't leave."

I tried to wiggle out from under the lion's paw, but his nails extended like a warning not to move.

"You should stay there for a while, you lost a ton of blood," Kelly said, coming around to the side of the bed and handing me a glass of water.

"I have to see Vincent. Is he here? It was an accident," I took the glass of water and leaned forward as far as Singh would let me so I could drink it. I didn't realize how thirsty I was until the water hit my lips. It was cold and felt amazing as it slid down my throat. "Thank you."

"Vincent isn't here, Lark," Kelly said, taking the empty glass from my hand.

I pushed the big paw off my chest and sat up. Singh grumbled but set his massive head down and went back to his nap. I sent out my senses and found Vincent right away. His light lit up like a spotlight in my mind. He was near the Neglinnaya River. I threw back the covers and looked around for my boots. I had to find him. There was something wrong with him. Durga rose along with her anger. She wanted to hunt Vincent.

"No," I said out loud, dropping my shoe.

"What's wrong?" Kelly said, coming back out of the bathroom with another full glass of water.

"Nothing, I'm sorry, I have to go. I pulled on my running shoes, grabbed the headlamp off the table and the glass of water out of Kelly's hand. I drank it on my way down the stairs. Singh was hot on my heels.

I headed for the front door, but the house human stopped me.

"Can I help you?" he asked.

"I need a car," I replied just as Ninel and Alex came around a corner.

"Lark, what's going on?" Ninel asked.

"I have to go get Vincent. Right now." My panic was growing. Durga wanted to hunt him, and I wanted to save him. If he killed someone, I would have to kill him, and I couldn't do that. Something was wrong with him.

"Ok, do you want me to get the team?" Ninel asked.

"There is no time. Let's go." Ninel grabbed keys from the human and sprinted behind me to a car parked in the driveway. Singh shifted as he leapt in the compact car's door and we tore out of the driveway and towards the Red Square.

I tracked Vincent. He was moving around in the sewers. I wanted to get as close to him as possible before we went down.

"I dislike this plan, Lark," Durga said with my mouth. She had never spoken to me with my own mouth before, and it shocked me. She relented control, and I replied out loud.

"I have to save him. There is something the matter with him. He isn't fallen."

"Perhaps you are too close to the vampire to see the truth," she replied.

"Holy shit," Drew wasn't here, but Alex filled in for him with the colour commentary.

"I can't Durga. He is mine. I won't let you destroy him!" I yelled. Durga didn't come back. She sat back down inside me like she would watch this play out.

"You have to help me," I said. She didn't reply, and the car fell silent for a few blocks.

"That was fucked up," Alex mumbled.

"Pull over!" I shouted, and Ninel slammed on the brakes. He pulled the car up onto the curb as car horns blared behind us, it was a no-parking zone, but I was sure Vaughn would handle a ticket if it meant saving his twin brother.

I jumped out of the car and raced to the closest sewer. The grate was heavy, but Durga loaned me strength, and I pulled it off with my hands before scurrying down the steel rungs and splashing down into the water in my running shoes. I turned and ran before anyone else made it down.

"Wait, Lark," Singh called before his voice turned into a roar. He could catch up. I ran through the puddles, my socks soaked and feet squelching on the bricks. I rounded a bend and climbed up into a higher drain. It fed out into the Metro. I stopped at the entrance. The tracks glistened in my headlamp. I listened but didn't hear any trains coming. I could feel Vincent's presence now. He was up ahead. Durga flashed my knife into my hand, and I threw it the opposite direction.

"Please?" I whispered. She didn't reply, but something flashed into my hand, and it wasn't my knife. It was a shell. A giant conch shell. Red eyes flashed up ahead, and I slowed to a walk. Now I was here, and I wasn't sure what the hell I was doing.

A low growl behind me alerted me to Singh presence. I took a deep breath. He was my will and determination. Well, he was Durga's, but I would borrow some of that will and determination.

"Vincent," I said as I got within a hundred feet of him. He rose from a crouch. I shone the light at his feet. It was another vampire. His neck a red ruin. That wasn't right. His eyes burned into me. They trailed down my body and back up to settle on my face after a momentary pause at the shell in my hand. When I blinked, Durga flashed me an image of the shell pouring sparkling magic into the tunnel.

I would have to trust her, because as I came to a stop, Vincent stepped over the vampire at his feet and bared his teeth at me in a menacing hiss.

I held up the shell and Durga took my voice, speaking words in a language I didn't recognize, but I assumed was Sanskrit. She chanted as he gained speed and raced towards me.

The flood of sparkling magic I had seen became real, and it slid across the ground of the metro tracks until it covered the whole area. As Vincent collided with the glitter, it wrapped him up, making him look like sparks from a campfire. There were no flames, but he yelled and then collapsed to the ground, not moving.

I panted, and tears welled in my eyes. Had I killed him anyway? I held my breath until his chest heaved a shuttering breath then I released the air from my lungs and ran the final steps towards him. Singh dashed in front of me before I reached him. He transformed into a man.

"Look with your senses. Do not trust your eyes alone," he said.

He was right. I took a deep breath and calmed myself. Then sent my senses forward. He was normal. He looked normal.

I moved past Singh and crouched be Vincent, rolling him onto his back. His face was bloody, but otherwise, he looked normal.

His eyes slid open. They were no longer red.

"Thank God," I muttered.

His arm came up, and he touched my face with the tips of his fingers, tracing a line from my temple to my chin.

"You are real," he said.

"Yeah."

"Um, Lark, we might want to move. Like, right now." I looked up to see a metro train coming up the tracks. Fast.

"Shit," I muttered as I hooked my arm under Vincent and yanked him up off the ground. He was heavy as hell, but once I got him up, he could move on his own. We raced back towards the tunnel I had come in from. The train was bearing down on us when Vincent picked me up and leapt into the sewer a moment before the train passed by. We lay there in a puddle catching our breath for a minute. Singh stood over us like we were a couple of idiots.

Vincent laughed and turned to face me. His lips found mine, and I didn't care I was soaking wet anymore.

He kissed me with so much emotion when he pulled away, I was breathing heavier than before.

His hands cupped my face, and his glowing eyes were all I could see. They weren't red and violent anymore. They were soft and beautiful.

"I'm sorry," he said.

"It's not your fault. Do you know who did that?" I asked.

He hummed. "Let's get out of here. I have a feeling Durga will want to hear the whole story."

Ninel splashed up to us as we stood and headed back out of the tunnels.

"What happened to you guys?" I asked.

"We lost you and took a wrong turn," Alex said before his eyes fell on Vincent. "Holy shit, it's the king."

"What?" Vincent asked.

As we walked back, I introduced Alex, who explained about the witch that gave him a prophecy hundreds of years ago.

"She said I would save the Lark and crown the king," he finished.

Vincent's eyebrows rose. "So, why do you think I'm this king?" Vincent asked. "Vampires don't have a king."

Alex looked back at Vincent again. "The same reason I knew she was the Lark. You glow."

Durga rushed forward and stared at Vincent through my eyes. He didn't glow, he looked normal.

"No one is glowing," she said sneering at Alex.

Alex's eyes got wide, and he moved over to the far side of Ninel.

I tried to get back into the driver's seat, but Durga wasn't finished. She continued to inspect Vincent. Singh strode forward and walked beside us. Durga used my hand to stroke his fur absent-mindedly as she studied the vampire.

When we got to the ladder that led to the street, Singh transformed into a man.

"You should not dismiss his words, Goddess," Singh said.

Durga locked eyes with Singh and reached out to rest her hand over his heart. "I dismiss nothing, but I will not believe blindly either." Then she retreated, leaving me to remove my hand from Singh's chest awkwardly. Singh bowed his head and then climbed the ladder, following Alex and Ninel.

I moved to follow Singh, but Vincent stopped me. He gave me one of his rare smiles and brushed my hair back from my face. It was wet from falling in the puddle and stuck to my cheek. I didn't feel the cold though, with his eyes tracing the features of my face.

"Thank you, for saving me. I thought I would rot there. I know what has happened to my brother now though. Vaughn is under the control of that beast."

"The buffalo demon did that to you?" I asked.

"Yes. Mahishasura. He has a witch too; a powerful one."

"Why are witches always involved? They need to butt out," I said.

Vincent laughed, and it echoed through the tunnels, he let me go and waved me up the ladder. He climbed up behind Ninel and me and replaced the grate. The remains of the parade still dotted the streets as we drove back to Vaughn's mansion. Vincent sat beside me in the cramped back seat of the car. His body against mine felt good. He was warm even though he smelled terrible. I rested my head on his shoulder soaked up the closeness I had been missing. I wanted to stay like that forever, but Durga flashed me an image of Elliana, lying dead beside Vaughn and the moment shattered. Sitting up, I looked out the window.

"What's the matter?" Vincent asked.

"Nothing," I said giving him a fake smile I hoped looked genuine. He didn't press the issue, and once we got back to the mansion, I hurried up the stairs to take a shower, while Vincent went off to find his brother.

Singh was hot on my heels and ducked into the bedroom before I shut the door, but then I locked it and slid down to the floor. Fuck.

I dropped my head into my hands and felt the first prick of a tear welling in my eye.

"Goddess will change her mind," Singh said. "If he is the king, she can't keep you from him."

"What does that even mean? Everyone keeps talking about the king, but the vampires don't have a king. I don't even know what that means. " There is only one king who would matter to Durga. The king of thunder. Indra."

The room turned red as Durga rose to speak. She stood and pointed her finger at Singh. "You will stop. The king has long since perished. A drought has taken over, and the desert sands blow in the hot wind."

"But do they blow for all of eternity? Or will our king rule once again and bring a new life to what was thought dead?"

Durga turned and stormed into the washroom. She slammed the door behind her and turned to look at the mirror. She braced her hands on the counter and moved closer to the glass.

"I do not believe he will return, Lark. This is foolishness. Continue our mission. Kill Mahishasura, and we will live forever, together. Your humanity will be your downfall."

My face was a stone mask. I didn't even look like myself in the mirror when Durga was present, but as I watched her retreat, my face smoothed into its usual shape and the red colour bled from my vision.

I needed to find out more about this king, but she was right. If I let Mahishasura carry on, who knows what kind of trouble he would get in to. He almost destroyed the earth last time he had free rein. I had to take care of him before he ruined everything.

I turned back and flicked on the shower, letting the water heat. My hair was drying, and it was crusty and gross with sewer gunk I didn't want to think about.

I washed it a few times before it felt clean and then stepped out and rooted through my suitcase. I found yoga pants and a hoodie and felt almost normal. As normal as I could get, anyway.

I came back out into the bedroom to find Singh sleeping as usual, and a plate of cheese and crackers was waiting for me on the table along with some juice and water. A few bites later, I sat on the floor and calmed my mind. I didn't want to fall into meditation and pop up in front of Shiva. Last time that happened he set his snake after me for disturbing him unnecessarily. So, I kept my eyes open as I slowed my breathing and heart rate.

I lay back and let my body sink into the floor. Let my libs feel like they weighed hundreds of pounds. Then I rolled over onto my stomach and pulled my knees up under my body. I pushed to my feet and rose in a slow uncurling of my spine. The pops and creaks felt good, and my lungs opened fully, taking a deep cleansing breath.

Once I was standing upright, I swept my arms above my head and went through the sun salutations routine. Curling through the windows, the evening sun welcomed me too. The corners of my lips curled up in a smile. I felt my calm place just beyond my fingertips as I swept my hands down to the floor, enjoying the stretch over my frame and through my lower back.

I continued, going through increasingly difficult poses until my body had a light sheen and my muscles felt loose and powerful.

Almost an hour later, I came to sit on the floor, legs folded in the lotus position. My hands rested on my knees and my spine straight. I felt so relaxed. I didn't even care if I accidentally interrupted Shiva and his damn snake. Then it occurred to me he might have information about this king, Indra.

I paused, trying to decide if I wanted the information or not, but Durga decided we wanted to talk to Shiva and sent me into meditation. She had shoved me out before, but never in, so my mind spun when I opened my eyes, and I was seated in front of the Hindu God. He blinked his eyes open and then raised an eyebrow. His snake slithered into his sleeve, disappearing from view.

"Why have you come? I thought we agreed you would leave me alone."

"Sorry. I have a few questions," I said, no idea what he was talking about.

"Oh, Lark. My apologies. I thought you were Durga." Shiva's snake peeked out of his sleeve and stuck its tongue out at me. His tongue flipping in and out of his mouth. Then wound his way out and up Shiva's arm to tangle in his hair and slip around his neck like a gross necklace.

I did not need to know about Shiva and Durga's marital problems, so I let that go. "I wanted to ask you about Indra.

"The king?" Why would you ask about him?"

"There is a vampire named Alex who we found in the tunnels. He said an old witch told him he would save the Lark and crown the king." I put air quotes around it with my fingers. It still sounded absurd. "Now he says Vincent is that king."

Shiva sat in silence. His snake even froze. Four eyes blinked at me. Shiva's third eye stayed closed, but I felt the uncomfortable swell of his magic.

“He has returned,” Shiva whispered.

CHAPTER TWELVE

"Who has returned? Are we still talking about this Indra guy?" I asked.

Shiva's eyes flicked back to me. "You must go, I have much to do!"

"Don't you dare!" I shouted as his snake came slithering down his arm and dropped to the ground on its fat belly with a plop. It didn't stop at my words, It kept coming towards me, hissing. I stood and took a step back.

* * *

I tripped and fell backwards, but strong arms caught me, and in a blink, I was back in the room in Vaughn's house, and Vincent was holding me.

"Are you ok?" he asked. His warm breath tickled across my cheek as he righted me.

"Yes. Sorry." I said turning around to look at him.

"Is everything all right?" The look of concern on his face made me melt. My resolve to focus on the job at hand wasn't very strong. I gave my head a shake.

"I just…" I glanced at Singh who was lying on the bed, his massive lion head on my pillow and his eyes open watching us.

"Shiva is just a jerk. Well, his snake is a jerk."

Vincent chuckled. "Come with me," he said, sliding his hand down my arm to take my hand.

"Where are we going?" I asked.

"I want to take you out for dinner and explain what happened. Durga will want to know."

"Yeah, the buffalo demon is all she is interested in now. Well, him and Vernon."

The smile fell from Vincent's face. He nodded. "Why don't you get changed and we can talk about it over dinner."

He turned and walked out the door. I sighed and rooted through my clothes. I had nothing nice to wear, so I walked down the stairs to find Kelly.

"Hey, Lark," she said as I entered the kitchen.

"Hey. Do you have something nice I could borrow? Vincent wants to take me out to dinner and I all I have is yoga pants and hip waders." I laughed.

"Sure, come with me," she said, drying her hands on a towel and leading me out of the kitchen. Her room was on the main floor. It was much smaller than the one I was staying in, but she had decorated in beautiful colours and floral prints. I had never decorated a room I stayed in. I always assumed it was temporary, but I would never be the type of person who decorated their room like this. This was the room of a happy person and seeing it reminded me I would not get my happy ending.

I borrowed a navy dress and a pair of heels to match and got changed before meeting Vincent in Vaughn's office.

"You look amazing," Vincent said. "You ready to go?"

His face lit up like I had never seen before. I doubt anyone from back home could tell him from his twin now. They had matching smiles. It was weird.

"Sure, let's go," I said, plastering a smile on my face. He took my hand and led me from the house.

The bad feeling in my stomach as we drove through the city didn't ease up. The street lights illuminated the roads, still flooded with commuters. They slowed our progress, and I felt the urge to get out and walk. Vincent seemed relaxed and at ease, but my muscles twitched and fingers tapped against my thigh.

I had been to a couple of restaurants in the city during my time here, but none compared to the one that Vincent drove me too. The valet parking was the first hint I would not be eating fast food. When we walked in, the restaurant had low lighting, with candles on the covered tables. A man in a suit spoke Russian to Vincent who replied in his mother tongue. I watched as they exchanged a few more words and the man led us to a private table in a back room. The walls were lush burgundy, matching the table clothes, but our feet clicked on the rich wood floors.

Vincent pulled out my chair, and I slid in as he pushed it in towards the table before taking his seat across from me. He smiled as the waiter spoke. I hadn't picked up any Russian that didn't have to do with the tunnels since I had been here. Knowing the words for sewers, metro and diggers didn't help in regular conversation. I also knew the Russian word for rat thanks to one run in with the giant sewer rat. Drew still says it was a beaver, but Alex, who always believed in the giant rats, was now telling the story of our run in like it was a near death experience.

As the waiter walked away, Vincent leaned forward and reached across the table, taking my hand in his.

He inspected my hand, rolling my fingers through his like he was thinking of something far away. It was a strange feeling to be sitting across from him and not have his attention. He was always so intent, his focus like a laser.

"You want to tell me about Mahishasura?" I asked, breaking the silence when it got too heavy.

His eyes refocused on me and he gave me a crooked grin. "Sorry." He let go of my hand and sat back in his chair, taking a deep breath.

"I wanted to talk to you about Vernon," he smiled, and that sick feeling crept back into my stomach. It wasn't Durga making me queasy, but she took notice when Vincent said the name.

"Ok," I said, stretching out the word like I wasn't sure it was ok.

"Listen, I know this will sound crazy, but I think Mahishasura is controlling him."
I gave him a doubtful look.

"Just hear me out. When you broke me out of the stasis or whatever that witch had me in, I felt like I was not myself. I was hungry, but not in control until you brought me back in the metro tunnel. The same thing might have happened to Vernon. I talked to Vaughn, and he agrees that it could be possible for you could bring Vernon back to us."

Vincent was so excited. He believed what he was saying.

"Listen, I wish that were true, but you and he were not the same. Vernon is of his right mind; you weren't. You were almost feral. Vernon is in control."

"Is he? How do you know?" he asked.

"He blew up three different buildings, Vincent. He killed people. Humans. Randy. That wasn't the work of a feral vampire. I felt his evil, Vincent, and if you are asking me to stop hunting him, I won't." Durga flashed in my eyes, confirming my statement. "We will avenge the one who killed our own," she said.

Vincent's face fell. "You can't kill him if you can save him."

"Who will save those he has already killed? I can't bring them back, can you?" Durga insisted. She settled down inside me again, content she had said her piece.

Vincent ran his hands through his hair and down his face. He sighed and bit his lip.

The waiter came to take our orders. I let Vincent order for me, but I wasn't hungry anymore. As the waiter walked away, Vincent's eyes bore into mine.

“Can I tell you a story?” he asked.

I nodded and took a sip of my water, wishing it was vodka.

"Before I moved to America, my brothers and I were wild. We had been vampires for so long that nothing thrilled us anymore. We hunted and..." he looked up at me. "...killed. Sometimes for no reason. Life would bore us, and so we would find trouble to stir up." He looked away like he didn’t want me to see the truth of his words. Durga already knew though. She has deemed him worthy of life, despite his past.

“One night, Vaughn and I were out drinking— alcohol, I mean — at a pub, when a woman walked in. She was fair and beautiful and so young. I wanted her. I wanted her youth, her beauty and her blood. Her scent rode the air behind her as she walked past me. Vaughn and I attracted attention wherever we went, but this woman, she didn’t come talk to us as the other woman did in the city. She sat, ignoring us and spoke to a man who was old and balding before she turned and left. Her eyes swept over me, but it was like I was invisible. Her eyes never landed on my features. During this time in history, people were poor and sick. They died young, and a healthy-looking man was hard to find. It was so strange to have a woman not interested in me or my brother that I had to follow her. I had to consume her."

He looked away again embarrassed.

I took another sip of my water and waited for him to continue. He told me he was not a good man or vampire before he left for America and that he left to change his ways, he hadn't given me details before.

"I followed her. The woman. Girl, really. She was young. Maybe 17." He shook his head. "She walked down the street and out of the village. I tracked her through the woods and across the meadows to a small cabin. It was just a one-room shack with smoke curling up into the night sky from a short chimney. I peeked in the window, hoping she would be alone, but she wasn't. Inside was a man, crippled with the plague. His cough rattled the cupboards. He was not long for the world. I figured I could speed the process if I took away the girl. She would die anyway since she was in proximity to the sick man. He was coughing up blood. That was the last phase before death.

I was about to open the door and have my dinner when a firm hand on my shoulder stopped me. It was Vernon. I asked him what he was doing, and he told me to look at the girl again. He begged me, so I looked closer. I saw nothing, but then her head turned, and I saw a flash of red. It was her, Elianna. About a year before she met my brother, and he helped her become a killing machine. I had heard the fable of the Durga, but had never seen her in life and thought myself invincible until that moment.

If I had gone in that cabin, she would have killed me before I even knew what she was. I would have been dead."

His hand reached out and took mine again. "I would never have met you."

Our waiter returned, and Vincent let go of my hand. He sat back, and the waiter set a plate of food in front of each of us.

When the waiter stepped away again, Vincent leaned in. "I'm just asking you to give him a chance. Heal my brother, the way you healed me and let my family be whole again."

I bit my lip. After hearing the story, I wanted his brother to be a good person. I wanted it so bad at that moment, but I knew, and Durga knew Vernon would never be a good person again. He was too far gone. No matter what Mahishasura did, the Vernon that Vincent knew no longer existed.

He was a ghost.

I nodded my head and picked up my fork. How do you tell someone you will kill their brother, no matter what good they have done in the past? Maybe it was for the best, at least this way Vincent would hate me and Durga would have her wish. No Lark and Vincent sitting in a tree.

We ate dinner in silence. Well, Vincent ate, I moved the food around on my plate. How could I eat?

After all the years of chasing his brother, Vincent chose now to have a change of heart. Figures.

When Vincent finished, we left the restaurant. I watched the city go by as we drove home. The street lights were blinding in contrast to the dark alleys of the city. I wondered how many people were in the sewers. I would have to go back there to find Mahishasura and Vernon. Sooner was better than later. Once I killed Vernon, I would have to leave. There was no way I could stay now.

My phone beeped as we walked back toward the front door of Vaughn's mansion. I pulled it out and checked the message. It was Frankie.

"I'm just going to make a call," I said, turning back towards the street.

"Ok," he said and continued into the house.

When I heard the house door close, I dialed Frankie's number, and he picked up on the first ring.

"Hey, sunshine," he said.

"Hey, I am in deep shit, Frankie."

"What's going on?" His tone changed from light and flirty to concerned in an instant.

"Vincent thinks I can save Vernon. He thinks if I use Durga's magic on him, I can bring him back and make him a good person, and I won't have to kill him."

"Why would he think that?" I called Frankie when we got Vincent back, but hadn't told him all the details, so I filled him in about Vincent throwing the steel spikes at me and then him drinking from the vampire in the metro and Durga giving me the power to bring Vincent back.

"So, he thinks Vernon is just under a spell?"

"Yes. I tried to tell him it wasn't a spell, but he couldn't hear me. He thinks I can make their family whole again. Durga won't let me leave Vernon alive. He may be under a spell, but he is fallen too. He would kill everyone in this city if I turned him loose."

"That isn't true, Lark." I startled and dropped the phone as I spun towards the voice behind me. Vincent stood there a scowl on his face.

"I'm sorry, Vincent. It is true," I said to him.

"Who are you talking to?" he asked.

"Frankie."

He laughed unkindly. "You conspire with the warlocks when their magic controlled my brother and me? I should have known. You stay away from my brother, Lark. I will find a witch to help him."

Durga rose so fast that Vincent was on his back, my knife to his throat before I even had a chance to digest his words.

"You do not tell me what to do. I keep the balance. I decide who lives and dies!" she roared.

The front door swung open, and Vaughn stood there.

"Durga, please. He didn't mean it. He's been through so much," Vaughn begged for his twin brother.

"This vampire dares to raise his voice and command Lark, as though she is a servant! You think she lives for your will? You have become too familiar with her. I will remind you only this once. Do not to trifle with her. You will mind yourself, or I will end you despite her interest in seeing you live."

Durga leapt to her feet and kicked open the gate at the end of the driveway, striding off down the street like we had somewhere else we could go. A light grumble behind us alerted me to Singh's presence. He walked behind but followed as Durga led us to a hotel several blocks away. Singh pulled out a credit card and got us a room, and we curled up on the large soft bed. He snored as I cried myself to sleep.

Everything had gone to shit.

CHAPTER THIRTEEN

I woke up to a scraping noise. I opened one eye and didn't recognize where I was at first. Then I remembered the look of anger and betrayal on Vincent's face.

I rubbed my eyes and tried to locate the noise instead of thinking about Vincent.

A purr rose through the room. Antique furniture accented the high-vaulted ceiling and beautiful soft blue wallpaper, including an old leather armchair that currently had a giant lion sitting in it. He was scraping his coarse tongue over a china plate on the table in front of him, holding it still with his paws. His big bristly tongue made short work of cleaning up the remains of whatever room service he had ordered himself.

"Did you order anything for me?" I grumbled.

He purred louder but didn't stop licking the plate. I rolled off the bed and into the bathroom to take a shower. The hotel supplied tiny shampoos and conditioners and individually wrapped soaps. I hadn't brought anything with me since Durga had stormed off without even picking up my phone off the driveway. Most likely broken now anyway, considering my track record with phones. I put back on the clothes I had slept in — the same borrowed navy dress I had worn to dinner with Vincent and had been wearing when everything went sideways but threw a plush housecoat over the top. It was white and had the logo of the hotel on it.

Back out in the room, there was a new serving cart, still covered and the smell of bacon emanated from it.

I took the top off and found one measly piece of bacon on an otherwise full plate.

"Did you eat my bacon?" I turned accusing eyes on Singh who paused in licking his paw for a moment before returning to his grooming.

Jerk.

"I picked up the fork and a plate of eggs and toast and moved to the small table. Completely lost to my thoughts about Vincent, I continued to shovel the food into my mouth until there was a knock at the door.

I froze, a fork full of eggs halfway to my mouth. Nobody knew I was here. I looked at Singh, but he tipped over on the bed and stretched like he didn't have a care in the world.

When whoever was at the door knocked a second time, I strode over and opened it up.

There, leaning against the door jamb, holding a bouquet of tulips, in his leather jacket and snug fit jeans, smelling of grease and leather, was Frankie.

"Oh my God, what are you doing here?" I squealed.

One corner of his mouth curled up.

"Are you happy to see me?" He asked, leaning forward.

Flinging my arms around his neck, I held on tight as his arms swept around me and he carried me back into the room.

"I can't believe you are here!" I said as he set my feet back on the ground and kicked the door shut behind him.

"Thought maybe you needed better company here in Russia after I heard your argument with Vinny."

"Shit," I said, shaking my head. Just like that, I went from joy to sadness. A sneaky tear slid out of the corner of my eye, and I bit my lip. I had been trying to stay strong, but now that Frankie was here, it was like the wall I built crumbled, and I fell apart.

"I'm sorry, Lark." Frankie wrapped me up in his arms again and rubbed his hand up and down my back. The smell of his leather jacket was comforting. Frankie had become so much more than a friend. Missing him these last several weeks or months, since I hadn't seen him much even when we lived in the same city, had made it clear. He was important in my life, even if he didn't say a word, his presence was important.

"I'm sorry," he whispered into my hair. The fact he could read my mind was still a bother, but it wasn't as big a problem as it once was. I wanted him to know how I felt. I wanted him to know how much I missed him and needed him.

"You should come home," he said.

"I wish I could, but I have to finish this. I have to take care of Vernon and Mahishasura."

"You know he doesn't look like what you think he does," he chuckled.

I had watched a cartoon video about the buffalo demon on-line, and he looked funny in my mind. I laughed, but Durga flashed an actual image of the monster on the back of my eyelids. God, he was disgusting looking. No mother could love that face.

"Thank you, Durga," I said, wishing I could go back to thinking of him as a cartoon villain.

Frankie laughed.

"Look, I think I want to get drunk today, then maybe tomorrow I will go back into the sewers, but I need a night off from all the drama. Will you escape the drama with me?" I asked Frankie.

"I would love to escape the drama with you," he replied. He reached into his jacket and pulled out a bottle of scotch. "I bought this at the airport, just in case."

Singh groaned on the bed and rolled over. I laughed, and Frankie unscrewed the top of the bottle before handing it to me. The liquor burned as it slid down my throat. I took a long sip and then coughed as I gave the bottle back to Frankie. He laughed and took a sip too.

It wasn't long before I had the TV flicked on and tuned to a romantic comedy — the only thing I could find in English. Frankie and I had shoved the sleeping lion to one side of the bed and cuddled together on the other side. Under the blankets, with the lights off watching the silly old movie, we laughed at the funny parts. When it got to the serious part, and the boy kissed the girl, Frankie tipped my head towards him and kissed me too. I was just drunk enough to enjoy it without thinking about any drama involving vampires. I was in the moment, and it was like magic.

His soft lips caressed mine as his hand traced my side making me shiver. He pulled me in close to him. Our bodies pressed together. His heart raced beneath my hand when I laid it on his chest, and our feet wiggled under the blankets until our legs entwined. I could hear my blood pumping in my ears mixed with the distant sound of the TV still blaring. Frankie's hand came up, and his fingers slid through my hair to cup the back of my neck. I came up for air, my breathing ragged and Frankie's lips traced my jaw and down my neck. My skin was on fire, and I thought my heart would explode.

"Oh, God,." I said.

Suddenly, a giant lion was standing on my hair.

"Shit!" I yelled, and the massive lion stepped over me, slipping his furry body between Frankie and me.

"Singh!" Frankie shouted. The lion wiggled until he made enough space for himself between us, then he huffed and put his head down on the pillow where I had been laying.

"You jerk," I said rubbing the back of my head where his giant paws had pulled some of my hair out.

Frankie laughed. I had to sit up to see him over top of Singh's mane, but Frankie's eyes were closed, and he was giggling like a crazy person. I couldn't help joining him, and weird snorting laughter forced its way out of me too. God, Singh was the worst pet and person ever.

It wasn't long before I shut off the movie and we all went to sleep. Frankie made his way back around to my side of the bed, but we kept it PG for Singh's sake.

Sleeping beside Frankie was like a luxury. His warmth and soft breath on my neck. It wasn't the same as sleeping with Singh. It was so much more.

"I'm glad," Frankie muttered. I rolled over to face him. His eyes were still closed. I craved the closeness he offered. He didn't hold himself back from me, and I didn't want to hold myself back from him. But the cold light of day sent doubts through my mind.

Frankie groaned and turned his face into the pillows, reading how my thoughts drifted.

"I'm sorry. You know it's complicated with Vernon, and Vincent is mad."

"I would love to be the only one you thought of all the time," he complained.

I ruined everything.

"No, you don't, Lark. You are perfect." He sighed, and his eyes traced my lips like he wanted to kiss them again. I wanted him too. I wanted to stay wrapped up in this blanket, in this hotel with this man and never leave. I wanted to have a normal life.

"I want that too," he whispered.

But I would never have a normal life. I would always be one step away from running out the door or across the world to chase after some buffalo or a vampire or who knows what.

Frankie smiled sadly. His place was with his coven. We both knew that. It didn't make it any easier.

I sighed. Life got in the way.

"Let's have breakfast. I can stay for a few more days, and I want to spend them with you unless you need to go hunting. I understand you know."

"No, let's order breakfast and spend the day here. The buffalo demon and Vernon will still be out there tomorrow." I rolled over and realized we had lost Singh.

"He left about an hour ago. You were sleeping. He said he would be back, but didn't say where he was going."

Well, he was a big boy, he could take care of himself.

I rolled off the bed and grabbed the menu and phone, then climbed back in beside Frankie.

I needed bacon and eggs. And maybe some fruit or something, My diet had been pretty shitty lately. Ninel had been handing me protein bars in the tunnels. I think Kelly was stocking his backpack with them for me. I spent so much time in the sewers, I was hardly at the mansion for meals.

After I ordered food for Frankie and me, I curled up in the blankets to wait. When there was a knock at the door, Frankie got up and went to answer it. He wasn't wearing a shirt, and his pants hung low on his hips, so his broad chest and toned abs were on display. I stared, it was the least I could do. He smiled at me and shook his head before he walked across the room to answer the door.

He pulled the door open, I expected room service, but instead, a furious vampire pushed past him and scowled at me.

"Looks cozy," he said, his eyes taking in Frankie's appearance and mine.

"What do you want?" I asked.

"I came to talk to you, I assumed you would be alone, but I guess I was wrong." He turned on Frankie. "Did you come racing in to save the damsel in distress?" his voice was cold, and his eyes blazed. "Or maybe you have been conspiring with the Mahishasura all this time?"

Frankie shut the door and raised his hands. He walked into the bathroom and closed that door behind him, leaving me to deal with the angry vampire. Chicken. I hoped he heard that.

"Seriously, Vincent? You are being unreasonable. Your brother is beyond redemption. Durga has already decided. I have decided. Whether he is under the control of Mahishasura is irrelevant. He is fallen. I can not save him."

"How do you know unless you try?" He hollered.

I rubbed my forehead and sat on the edge of the bed. His anger didn't even touch me. Durga was so close to the surface, I felt more like her than myself. My back straight, I raised my chin and locked eyes with him. His resolve to save his brother was as clear as my resolve to end him. This wouldn't end well. I couldn't.

I tried to think of a way around this. There was a good chance Vernon would run, anyway. Maybe I would never catch him.

"OK, Vincent. I will try to save your brother."

His shoulders relaxed first and then a moment later he crumpled to my feet.

"Thank you, Goddess."

"Do not thank me," Durga said, shocking me. She was so close that she barely moved when she took over. "I would rather be rid of his sickness, but Lark does not wish to hurt you. Do not thank me. If your brother is not immediately remorseful, I will slay him against Lark's wishes and lose no sleep."

Vincent nodded, biting his lip. His eyes were still downcast. I wanted to reach out to him, but Durga wouldn't let me move my hands. She and I may get along, but she was still the one in control. She decided if I lived or died as much as she decided among the vampires. It was a depressing thought.

Durga whisped away and left me to my own devices which meant that when Frankie came back out of the bathroom, the sight of my hand in Vincent's hair and his head in my lap as he knelt at my feet greeted him.

His face said everything.

I was the worst kind of shit.

CHAPTER FOURTEEN

"It's fine, Lark. I'm just going to go, ok?" Frankie said, picking up his shirt off the floor and pulling it over his head.

Vincent rose to his feet. "I'm leaving," he declared too.

"Just… shit." I said as I followed them to the door. Vincent reached out to open the door, glaring at Frankie, when the door burst open, and Singh walked in.

"Honey, I'm home," he said with a grin. "What are all these people doing in your bedroom?" he asked, mocking horror as he covered his mouth with his hand. I hated him more at that moment. I flipped him off, and he chuckled before crossing the room and flopping onto the bed as he shifted into a lion.

When I turned back around Vincent and Frankie had left. I crossed back to the bed and threw myself down on it beside Singh. Maybe I could just go back to sleep and wake up all over again. I was trying to figure out how I could have handled the situation better when there was a knock at the door. I jumped up and strode across the room, flinging the door open.

Outside the door was a small oriental woman pushing a cart with the smell of bacon wafting from it. I stepped back, and she pushed the cart in before she turned on her heel and walked back out again.

"Thank you," I called, closing the door and turning back to get to the food before Singh stole all the bacon again.

As I munched and Singh licked his plate clean, I decided. "We should get back to the tunnels."

Singh stopped licking his plate and looked up at me, a tiny blip of his tongue sticking out between his whiskered lips.

"I need to get this over with," I said. He licked his lips. "Be a human for two seconds so I can talk about this. You are the worst embodiment of my will and determination ever."

Singh huffed and shifted.

"Well excuse me. I thought we were having breakfast. From now on I'll be ready to jump to work at a moment's notice, but if I pass out from lack of food, it will be your fault."

"You ate three helpings of bacon and then half of mine."

"Fine, you need waterproof clothes though. Let's go shopping first." Singh pulled out Vincent's credit card. Who knows how he got his sticky paws on it, but I would not complain. I would never get the million dollars Vincent owed me if I killed his brother and according to Durga, we wouldn't have a choice.

"We could go back to the mansion. We don't have to stay here," I reminded him.

"Kelly won't make me bacon," he whined, leaning back in his chair.

The laugh jumped out of my mouth before I even had time to acknowledge it was coming. "You are such a cat. Follow the food."

He grinned, then stole my last piece of bacon.

As I was getting my boots on, there was another knock at the door. Singh opened it to reveal Ninel, Vilen and Alex.

"Hey, guys. Come to join the party?" Singh asked as they filed in.

"We heard there might be a hunting party," Alex said. The wall of muscle behind him smiled, their eyes twinkling at the prospect of violence.

I finished pulling on my boots, and we left the hotel. Parked in front was the giant hummer, full of all our gear. I guess we didn't need Vincent's card.

We went back to the place we found Vincent.

Entering the tunnel system in a different area, I was completely turned around. Alex had a hand-drawn map of the tunnels around the Red Square, but the small tunnel wasn't on the map, so we had to approximate its location.

The entrance was a grate in the park, and there was no ladder down, so Ninel tied a rope around my waist and lowered me down. The rope cut into my sides and pinched the skin under my arms. I spun a few times before my feet touched down in the water below.

Singh jumped down after me with a splash, and the vampires dropped into the water with a splash, one at a time. It took a while to find our bearings in the tunnel. The sewers looked the same once you were in them in this area. Faded red brick and mortar arched over our heads. Hard water deposits etched the walls, and as we moved towards the old mine, the stalactites grew longer. The meters of stone and soil above our heads muffled the sound of traffic above. When we found the turnoff to the mine, I oriented myself and pointed up.

Singh stood by the wall beneath the drain and lifted me so I could pull myself up into the tight space. The crawl through the narrow sewer was drier than the last time, and I paused at the grate below the highway and tried to send out my senses. I didn't like going in there without being able to sense anything, but it was still a dead zone — a complete black hole. I continued, and as I tumbled down, I swung my headlamp around, it was, thankfully, empty. I wasn't ready to meet up with Mahishasura yet, but I worried that Vernon had already left the tunnels or even left Moscow. He stayed nowhere long.

I swept my headlamp around the room. The wall where Vincent was pinned like a butterfly was bare except for the holes in the wall that the stakes had been driven into and the dark stains running down from them. A sharp pain in my stomach reminded me what had happened in the room. I put my hand to my stomach and closed my eyes. Durga flashed on my eyelids, her reminder of the pain Vincent had caused. Like that would be enough to change my mind about him. He wasn't in his right mind when he did that. Durga vanished, disgusted at my resolve not to blame Vincent.

"Look at this," Ninel said from the other side of the cavern. I walked over and found markings on the wall.

There was a straight line and below the line were curls and dashes. It looked like writing, but I didn't recognize it.

Durga flashed forward, turning my vision red, she inspected the markings. Words poured from my mouth in a strange language, and a glow radiated from the marks. We all took a step back, and the glow expanded to cover the whole wall. A sharp squealing sound emanated from the smooth cement and the light split upwards from the floor and then across the ceiling and back down again in the shape of a large garage door.

I held my breath and waited. The magic was thick and palpable.

The cement wall faded until it disappeared revealing a second cavernous space. As my headlamp illuminated the space, several pairs of red glowing eyes reflected back. A low growl came from Singh behind me. A hissing noise rose from the depths of the shadows beyond the new doorway.

"Oh shit," I whispered. A loud squeak shattered the silence. Several more followed and the red eyes launched towards us. My headlamp caught on a furry body about the size of a large cat just before it cleared the door and jumped for my face. My knife was in my hand in an instant, and in the next, it was slicing through fur and flesh until it scraped across the bone. The animal screamed and fell to my feet. Its long, skinned tail quivered a second before it was still. I didn't have time to be disgusted by the rat because dozens more flooded out of the doorway. The sounds of fighting filled the cavern. Singh's roar deafened me as another rat launched towards me. I swung my knife down again and sliced across its neck before it got to me. The next rat was swifter and got its foul teeth into my arm. Its breath was like death as it filled my nose and churned my stomach. It bit down and held on. I shook my arm as another rat grabbed onto my leg. Durga, having had enough, pushed me out of the way and took over the job of killing giant rodents. She sliced and diced the rats as they came forward. I had never seen so many rats, and they continued to flood the tunnel. The blood sprayed, and the dying animals screamed. They weren't magical creatures but to be acting so out of character they had to be under the influence of magic. I was willing to bet that the witch who had captured Vincent was behind this disgusting display.

The guys behind me cursed and roared, fighting off the gross sewer rodents. I left Durga to do the worst of the work.

She kicked a rat sneaking up on me while she stabbed another. Blood sprayed and coated my headlamp, sending me into darkness. I could make out the figures scurrying around me like I was a rock parting the river of fur and rat tails.

The viscous liquid dripped into my mouth, and I sputtered and spat as the last of the giant rats moved by. I swung around and watched as they scaled the wall and out the drain, we had entered from. I reached up and cleared the blood from my headlamp and made sure everyone else was ok. Singh had a dead rat in his mouth. He shook it one last time before dropping it with a plop. Gross.

"That was disgusting," Alex commented. He wiped his knife on his shirt and tucked it back into his boot.

Ninel and Vilen stepped between the rat bodies and moved towards the doorway to the new cavern. I swung back around and illuminated the space with my headlamp. It was now empty of rodents. We crept forward. The floor was coated in squishy rat poo. The stench was overpowering, burning my eyes, and I prayed there was an exit on the far side. It was so much darker like the room was full of fog. I put my hands out and felt someone's back, but I couldn't be sure who it was because my vision had gone to zero.

"Lark, I don't like this," Alex said. Singh's huff alerted me to his presence at my side a moment before his furry mane touched my hand. I threaded my fingers through his fur and stepped forward. Durga stayed close to my surface. Her presence, along with Singh, bolstering my confidence, but I was sure something would jump out at me from the darkness. I was fine with monsters, but I wasn't fine with them sneaking up on me.

I reached up and wiped at my headlamp again, but the darkness wasn't because of a dirty light. It was this place. It was dark magic that hung in the air. I put my hand out again, but could no longer reach the back in front of me.

"Ninel?" I whispered. When I got no reply, I tried again. "Ninel?" I called louder. My fingers were still threaded in Singh's fur. I held on, his low growl, almost inaudible, rumbled under my hand. I wanted to turn and run. Leave and never come back. The air grew thick until I was struggling to take each step and each breath was laboured. I knew it was magic, but that didn't stop the desire to flee.

I took another few steps with my arm outstretched before I felt the familiar back of Ninel's jacket. Grabbing onto it, I let him lead me through the dark. It was several more steps of total blackness before my headlamp seemed to come back to life and fight through the magical darkness to illuminate an immaculate subway line.

This was nothing like the dingy one that took people from one end of the city to the other. This one was mint.

We found Metro 2.

CHAPTER FIFTEEN

The ceiling in this tunnel was not like the others. It was square and modern. It wasn't wet and fractured or dirty. Tracks gleamed under recessed lighting that illuminated the dim space. The sound of feet on the cement floor of the tunnel alerted us to people coming, and we all turned. Soldiers armed with semi-automatic weapons came towards us, their guns drawn and pointed. They wore pristine uniforms and looked like commandos in their helmets, fatigues and boots. Masks and goggles covered their faces. As they marched closer, they yelled in Russian. Their voices echoed through the tunnel, and I watched as Alex, Ninel and Vilen got on their knees and laced their hands behind their heads. I stood and waited beside Singh. The men surrounded us and continued yelling. Singh yawned, and a few of the men backed up, but they didn't stop yelling.

"Just get on the ground, Lark," Alex said, his voice rising over the horde of soldiers.

I relented and got to my knees. Some soldiers approached us, pulling our hands behind our backs and cuffing them. The rest kept them kept their weapons trained on us. Singh sat down and yawned like it was the most boring day. The fact he wasn't a lion skin rug yet was strange. It was as if they were expecting us and knew what Singh was.

"Stand up," the man behind me said in English once he cuffed me.

They marched us through the tunnels to a set of stairs leading up to a metro station. The markings painted on this platform were the same as the ones civilians used all over the city. Once on the platform, they pressed us into a freight elevator which took us up into a building. According to my approximation, we were under the Kremlin.

The elevator door opened, and they ushered us down a long corridor and into a massive room I recognized as the grand Kremlin from photos in the travel brochure in the hotel. It was a building within the fortress in the city's center. The floor was ornate and glossy in gold and blue patterns. Our feet tapped off the surface, sending sound around the vaulted ceiling.

The arched walls had decorative gold and red engravings, and the ceiling matched the walls and pillars. Ahead a set of doors stood open. Above them, stylized pictures of men on horseback in long cloaks and warriors with spears decorated the wall.

Lining the sides of the immense space were golden chandeliers with hundreds of tiny bulbs. They matched the sconces on the walls, and every light glowed like a Christmas trees.

We walked through the set of doors, beneath a carving of an eagle. Inside they turned us to the left and marched through a hidden doorway in a bookcase.

"Good evening," a stern man in a military uniform said. He stood behind his desk, his sharp eyes taking in our ragtag appearance. He was in his late 60s, but his graying beard didn't make him looks soft. It made him look coarse and sharp like the blade of my knife.

"Hey, how's it going?" I said, and he scowled at me.

He walked around the desk, his eyes still on me like I was the biggest threat. Everyone in the room dwarfed my five-foot frame, but with Durga on my team, he was right to watch me.

Singh stepped in front of me and huffed at the army general.

The man sneered at the lion but stopped moving towards me.

"What were you doing in the metro?" the general asked, pacing in front of us.

"Hunting giant rats," I said. One soldier behind me snickered but bit off the laugh before the general's eyes shot up to pick out the responsible party.

The door behind us opened, and I heard a set of dress shoes on the parquet floor. I knew who was back there; I didn't need to turn around.

"Good evening, General." Vincent's sharp voice rang through the room.

The General knocked his heels together and saluted. I changed a look and discovered Vincent dressed in as a Russian General too, except he was higher in rank, based on the number of people saluting him. I wondered if he was taking his brother's official place at the moment. It was doubtful he would have army rank after centuries in America, but he looked like his brother dressed up as he was and he had let his accent come back into his voice. He looked amazing. I had never thought of myself as someone who liked a man in uniform, but this was something else. This was the potent combination of Vincent and the power he commanded.

That was the moment I saw it — the glow that Alex had said flickered around Vincent like a halo. A golden light.

I stared at him in awe. He was speaking in Russian now, and I didn't understand a word, but it didn't matter when his eyes locked with mine and my blood boiled beneath my skin. My face heated and his lip curled into a small smile.

The guards all put up their weapons at a few more words, and they stood down. Singh huffed and sauntered towards the door they had led us through, his tail twitching back and forth.

"Let's go, Lark," Ninel said, gripping my elbow and steering me past drool-worthy Vincent. I could almost feel Durga's eyes roll and didn't care. He was stunning. His broad shoulders and well-cut uniform. His cap was sitting jauntily on his head.

As I walked past, his eyes followed me until I was around the corner. A guard led us back to the freight elevator.

"What did he say?" I asked Ninel as we went down the elevator.

"He told them you were part of a special team that was hunting a dangerous fugitive. They were to let you complete your sweep and stay out of the tunnels until further notice."

"That's handy," I mumbled.

"It's definitely handy. We have full access. Let's go find the fallen one," Ninel spoke in the vampire soft tones, below human hearing.

"Do you think he's fallen?" I asked in the same voice. It had taken me a while to get the hang of speaking below human hearing, but I was confident now I could do it without being heard. Drew had helped me master it, the thought reminded me I was missing a team member.

"Where is Drew?" I asked in a normal voice.

"I'm sorry, Durga, I have not seen him," Ninel's face was solemn.

Durga rose to the surface and smiled at the vampire before she receded.

"What is the story with you and Durga?" I asked him in the quiet voice. The elevator opened, and we stepped off, leaving the guard behind.

We walked down the steps back onto the rail line as Ninel told me the story.

"Six hundred years ago, Durga walked the earth in the body of a woman named Kittur. She was a warrior princess in a time of men. She rode her horse and battled full armies. I was just a gladiator, fighting men for the entertainment of kings. But through the city, I heard whispered stories about Kittur, and my curiosity grew until one day I got on my horse and rode. The journey was several weeks. I had heard of the legend of the Durga but wasn't sure how to believe it until I saw her face and her eyes flashed red. Then I knew she was the Goddess. I dropped to my knees before her. I was just a human, but I pledged allegiance to her on that day, swearing I would fight for her until my last breath."

"She led me to war many times, always keeping me close to her. We battled against monsters and men. She kept the balance, no matter which way it swung, she pushed it back to the center again."

"Watching her swing a sword from the back of her horse was the most magnificent thing I have ever seen," he said, smiling at me. His face was so open when he spoke. "I devoted my life to her, and when I died, she brought me back, immortal, so I could continue to serve her."

My eyes went wide. "She made you a vampire?"

"Yes, it was the greatest day of my life. One I will never forget."

His words echoed through the tunnel and silence descended on us. Our feet scuffled over the cement in a steady rhythm.

Durga made him a vampire.

She pushed forward and spoke. "I would do it again in a heartbeat. My bravest warrior." She reached out, squeezed his hand, and then retreated inside me.

I felt like I had intruded on a private moment. Their history was so long. Beyond my comprehension. I studied Ninel's profile as we walked through the tunnel. His broad nose and hardened features certainly made him look like a gladiator.

I was still studying him when Alex spoke. "We should look through some of these smaller tunnels."

I dragged my eyes away from Ninel and took in the rest of the space. I could see dozens of tunnels coming off the main one, in both directions. Alex was still talking about the tunnels, so I tuned back into the conversation.

"The word is that the main tunnel goes from one end of the city to the other. There are also stories about living quarters and cities down here."

"Some of those stories are true," I spun around to see Vincent behind us. My heart stuttered a second before I found my words.

"What are you doing here?" I asked.

"Making sure you don't end up in a Russian prison."

Durga shot forward at his words. Her anger was palpable.

When my eyes bled to red Vincent smiled. "Good. I wanted to say something to you, Durga," he said. "Lark agreed to help my brother. I don't want you taking over and trying to kill him before she does that."

"You do not control me. Nor do you control Lark. She may worry about your feelings, but I do not. I care for the balance, and your brother has fallen. He will not stop his rampage, and I will not suffer his darkness to walk the earth."

"That's your choice I suppose, but you should know I have Drew."

He let the words hang in the air. The tension grew as Durga processed the implications.

"Where is my Drew?" she asked, her voice a low growl.

"He is fine. I've just kept him safe for you so that you might consider the plea for my brother's life."

"You attempt to blackmail me? You think I will fold to your will just because you hold one of mine?"

Durga launched herself forward and slid our knife into Vincent's stomach. He fell over backwards, landing on the cement. Durga rode him down and then brought her face close to his.

"I could kill you and then kill your brother and all the vampires you have ever made. I could destroy your whole bloodline and then every vampire who walks the earth." Her words echoed through the place, and her heaving breaths were the only noise for several tense moments. I didn't dare move. I prayed she wouldn't kill Vincent here in this tunnel. He was being an idiot. This was crazy.

"Please?" he rasped.

"Your love for humanity and your family is the only reason my knife is not in your neck right now Vincent. I will not abide this. You will leave this place and go back to your twin. Stay with him while Lark and I do this thing that we must do. We will try to save your brother, but this is not the way. You are too close and can not be reasonable."

Vincent nodded. He still hadn't tried to move; he let Durga talk.

"You will also never threaten one of mine again. Drew belongs to me." She bared her teeth at him as though she was a vampire. I supposed she was kind of the baddest vampire of all, except she didn't drink blood.

Durga twisted our knife, and Vincent groaned "Yes, Durga."

Singh huffed, breaking the tension.

Durga rose, leaving the knife in Vincent's stomach. He grabbed hold of it, but she put her boot on the hilt. He groaned. Blood was spilling out of the wound and soaking the beige uniform.

"You will not blame Lark if she must kill your brother because he is fallen. I am not wrong, but I will give him one chance. He will have one moment before I decide, no more. This is the gift I give you because of Lark. I would not give this boon if not for her.

"Thank you, Goddess," he whispered.

She removed my boot from the hilt of the knife and settled back inside me, leaving me in charge again.

Vincent rose. His face a mask. I wanted to see him smile but knew I wouldn't see it anytime soon. Maybe never after today. Vincent had turned from chasing down his brother to wanting to save him so fast, I still couldn't believe he was this determined. I searched his face for some sign of the softness I used to see when he looked at me, but it was all cold and hard. Swallowing the desire to fix this any way possible, I watched as he dropped my knife and turned, striding back down the tunnel.

"Holy fuck that guy has a death wish," Alex whispered.

"Not news," I replied turning away from Vincents receding back. He had pushed Durga more than once and even tried to get me to kill him once when Durga first appeared. I thought of all the times I sparred with him, and he let it get way too far. I wondered if Vincent didn't value his life. That was a thought for later. We had work to do, and I wanted to get it over with as soon as possible. I needed out of these tunnels and out of this city. The level of crazy was off the charts.

I sighed and followed along behind the guys who had picked up the conversation in Russian. Too busy with my thoughts to join in any way, I followed them until I felt a tug. I stopped walking, but only Singh noticed.

"Hey guys," I said.

They swung around and looked at me.

"There is something down here." I pointed to the tunnel beside me. It wasn't like the pull of a vampire. It was something else.

Something dark.

CHAPTER SIXTEEN

The tunnel was dark; there were no lights in this section. We crept forward guided by our headlamps, but the shadows were thick. It was like the shadows in the cavern between where we found Vincent and where we came out in Metro Two. So far Metro Two didn't seem like the hidden underground city they rumoured it to be, but something strange was in this tunnel. I felt eyes tracking my movement, skimming over me and trying to pull me apart. The hair rose on the back of my neck and goosebumps lifted on my arms. Singh slid in beside me, his whiskers brushed against my waterproof pants, making a whisper sound in the stillness. We all walked on quiet feet.

Something flashed through my headlamp beam. I tried to track it as it moved, but it was fast.

"What was that?" Alex whispered.

Singh growled so low it was inaudible, but I felt it vibrate from him. The echo of unsheathing knives and swords broke the silence.
Turning my head, I tried to get a map of the space, there was another tunnel going off to the right, and ahead the tunnel kept going farther than my light could reach. This place was a maze. I hoped my batteries were good. Being in here in the pitch black was not on my list of 'fun things to do and see in Russia.'
Wings flapping and the rustling of feathers filled the quiet. It was low at first, distant, but then it grew like a freight train.
Vilen yelled, and I turned to see him surrounded by birds a moment before they crashed into me. Their sharp beaks stabbed at my face, and their nails tore at my hair. I smacked the small birds away. Their delicate wings flailed as they tumbled to the ground. The dark magic clung to them, and I knew the witch was controlling them.
"Run," Alex yelled.
I didn't think twice. I threw my hands over my head and ran blindly down the tunnel. The birds flapped after me as I ran. The sound of the guy's feet pounding behind me told me I wasn't running alone. I glanced back for a second to make sure everyone was with me, but before I could get a head count, I was falling.

I let out a squeak before I collapsed to the ground in a heap. Groaned, I pushed my face off the dirt, rolling over onto my back to count the injuries. There was a sharp stabbing pain in my leg. I bit my lip to keep from crying out. Reaching out, I ran my hand blindly down my leg until I came to a place it bent at ninety degrees to the left. Hot wet blood pooled inside my waterproof pant leg, confirming I had done more than a little damage. The fact no one had fallen on top of me was an upside to the situation. I stared into the dark hoping my eyes would adjust, but without my headlamp, it was all just black. I reached around behind me, and my fingers whispered over the strap for my headlamp but knew before I even tried that I broke it. My forehead had a welt the approximate size and shape of the lamp.

"Lark, you ok?" Alex called from the top of the hole I fell in.

"Yeah," I muttered. I didn't bother yelling. I felt the stabbing pain in my ribs. It would need a few minutes to heal, and they would have heard my whisper, anyway. Durga's healing was already working. I felt the bone in my leg snap back into place. Vomit rose in my mouth, but I swallowed it back down. I had not vomited once in Russia, and I would leave the city the way it was when I came. Lark puke free.

I lay back on the cement floor to wait for my leg to finish healing. The cold seeped in, and I shivered. Half from the temperature, but some from shock too. Or maybe blood loss. My foot was swimming in blood now inside my boot.

I felt a breeze and heard a light thud before Singh's comforting purr motor started.

“Hey, buddy,” I whispered as he lay beside me. He dropped a drooled-on flashlight on my chest and then set his head on my shoulder. His heat permeated my clothes and warmed me. Closing my eyes, I tried not to think about anything but knew I needed to get moving. I was positive now that the witch responsible for the magic in these tunnels was nearby and I didn’t want to sit and wait for her to bring her magic down on me again.

I moved around, testing my leg and ribs. There was no immediate stab of pain. So, I clicked on the flashlight and pushed off the floor. I slid out from under the lion's head and sat up. Singh curled around my back and supported me until the room stopped spinning. The guys had been arguing in Russian for several minutes when I stood and got a good look at the hole I was in. The edges were ragged, like a sinkhole, but the ground was smooth like I had fallen into a sub-level. I didn't think it was an accident though. This was purposeful. Anyone who knew anything about Durga would know this wouldn't stop her. She flittered about in my stomach, angry at the delay. If the goal was to tick her off, consider the objective achieved.

"Hey, guys!" I yelled over the Russian's arguing.

"Hey, Lark. We are just discussing how to get you out of there," Alex replied.

"Ok, cause it doesn't look like there is any way out except up," I said.

The walls on two sides were smooth like a man-made tunnel, but the front and back had caved in with rock and dirt. The hole was about forty feet up.

"Do you guys have a rope?" I asked after inspecting the hole I was in.

"We do, but not enough. We could send someone back to get more rope." Alex didn't seem sure about that idea. It was a long way back, and we would be sitting ducks in the meantime.

I looked at Singh. He stood up and walked in front of me, sidling up like he did when he rubbed his face on my stomach, but instead stopped and lay at my feet.

Durga pushed me to get on the lion. I didn't understand why that would help, but Durga insisted, so I sat on Singh, and he wasted no time. He stood and walked to the rubble wall like I weighed nothing. Then he reared back and leapt ten feet up onto a boulder. I grabbed onto his thick mane and wrapped my legs around his waist. His talons tore into the dirt and stone as he leapt straight up the wall from the narrow edge of rock to a piece of fallen cement.

If I hadn't been hanging on for dear life, I would have almost enjoyed the feeling of being launched into space. Maybe not. But when Singh made the last leap and landed softly beside Alex, I found a new respect for my lion friend. He was more than a lazy house cat sometimes.

I slid off the lion's back and looked around the tunnel. The birds had disappeared. The guys had small scratches and scrapes on their faces, all healed thanks to vampire healing, but drops of dried blood lingered, marking the places the little birds had dug in.

I turned back towards the hole in the floor. There was a narrow path around the hole on one side.

The darkness was emanating from the far end of the tunnel. Or somewhere past the hole.

I took a deep breath and the first squishy step towards the small path. The blood in my boot was uncomfortable and growing colder by the minute, but I had to end this.

Alex jogged past me, to cross the path around the hole before me. He flashed me a quick smile and then pressed up against the wall and crept along to the far side. I followed his lead, inching my feet along. The flashlight somehow made it up out of the hole with Singh and me. I shone it down the tunnel when we got past the hole in the floor but still couldn't see the end or anything for that matter. Whatever this witch was using to hide was powerful magic. I passed Alex, not wanting to leave him in the lead if we ran into something more powerful than a vampire. I knew from the stories Vincent told me that witches and warlocks could kill vampires and had hunted them long ago before they signed the treaty.

The shadows got thicker, swallowing the light beam, the farther we walked. I felt the push to turn around again, but it was an old trick now. I recognized it for what it was. Magic. I also had magic, thanks to Durga and pressed on.

"Lark, do you think it is much farther?" Alex rasped into the eerie silence.

I was about to reply when I heard something. It was a quick whizzing noise. Strong arms shoved me out of the way, knocking me to the ground. Then there was a gurgled noise followed by a thud.

I crawled across the ground and grabbed the flashlight that flew from my hand and swung it back to find everyone on the ground, but Alex lay on his back, his chest bowing to the ceiling as blood gushed from the wound on his neck. I crawled to him and pressed my free hand to the wound. It hadn't severed his spine, but I could see the glistening white of the bone for a second before blood covered it.

"Shit," I said, looking around for what had done this. Ninel and Vilen rose to their feet, and beyond them, I saw a sword laying on the ground. It was intricate like a piece of art, not a weapon any of the team was using. It had almost decapitated Alex.

Durga rose and spread heat into my hand until it was so hot, I wanted to let go of Alex. He screamed and thrashed on the ground, my scream joining his. It seemed to go on forever, but finally, the heat dissipated and I could remove my hand. Durga had healed Alex, again. He would have recovered on his own, but it seemed she had taken a shine to the strange vampire.

"He is mine," she whispered directly to me. It was a strange and personal way for her to communicate. One she had only used once before. It felt like talking to myself. Like the two of us were one, and I wasn't sure how to feel about it, but at the moment I was happy she had saved Alex. I was tired of this witch's tricks. It was time for action.

Durga agreed.

I stood and raised my arms, hoping Durga would play

along. Of course, she did, the little drama queen.
She divided my arms until I stood in the tunnel in her image and with all the rage I could muster I screamed.
"Come forth you filthy magic wielder. I will not abide your games."
Our skin glowed a soft green, illuminating the darkness that tried to absorb us.
All around, etchings on the walls appeared. The words were in Sanskrit and Durga scanned them before scoffing.
"You think your God will save you from me?" She snorted. "Come forth or suffer my wrath!"
I was sure the witch would suffer our wrath anyway, but what slunk out of the shadows made my jaw drop.
A tiny boy of no more than six stood before us. My breath caught in my throat. His hair was scraggly and dirty and his clothes tattered. He sniffled and wiped his nose. Durga rose to stare at him too. His small frame shook in the cold tunnel, and he wrapped his arms around himself. He kept his eyes trained on his shoes. They were two sizes too big, and his bare ankles showed between the tops of his shoes and the bottom of his too-small pants.
"Who are you?" I whispered, stepping forward.
Singh blocked me from going closer. It was just a small boy though. I couldn't imagine how he got down here,

but he looked lost and cold. I wanted to scoop him up and take him away.

"Um, Lark?" Alex said from behind me. I didn't turn around. The little boy's blue eyes caught mine and I couldn't turn away. It was like he was my little boy, so beautiful and perfect and everything I had ever wanted. His dark hair was an exact match for my own, but his eyes. They were Vincents. As soon as the thought entered my mind, I could see other signs of Vincent. The shape of his nose and his lips. The corner of his mouth curled in a tentative smile and I was lost. My heart stopped in my chest.

I squatted down and opened my arms to him. The smile on my face was genuine. I wanted to care for this little boy and make him so happy. I wanted to watch him grow and flourish and never see him cold or dirty again.

"Durga!" Ninel shouted from behind me.

"Come here, it's ok," I said, ignoring the vampire behind me. Durga watched through my eyes, her love for him as strong as my own, but when the boy looked frightened, she slid away and let my eyes bleed back to their usual chocolate brown.

Singh huffed, startling the little boy. My little boy. I shoved the tiger out of the way and scowled at him. "Do not scare my boy," I said, my voice more like Durga's than my own. I turned back to my sweet boy and smiled again. "You see? It's OK. Mommy's here." I opened my arms again to the boy. He took a tentative step, then another.

I held my breath, but a moment later he scurried forward and was in my arms. His warm hands wrapped around the back of my neck and his sweet smell filled my nose.

"I love you, Elliot," I whispered. The moment was perfect, and I closed my eyes. Nothing else mattered as long as Elliot was in my arms. I stood and lifted him off the ground. He was so small and fragile, like a tiny bird that needed my protection.

"LARK!" someone yelled behind me, I tried to turn my head, but someone knocked me down as a knife shot through the air, my knife, I realized, towards my head. Instead, as I crashed to the ground, the blade ricocheted off the wall behind me. I sprung up to look for Elliot, but he had disappeared.

"Elliot!" I yelled. Everyone was just standing there staring at me. "Find him! Where did he go?" I screamed. I turned and then ran up and down the tunnel.

"Elliot!"

"Durga!" Ninel called again. I couldn't stop to talk to him. I had to find Elliot.

Someone attacked me from behind. Steel arms circled my

waist, lifting my feet from the ground.

I screamed and kicked, trying to get free and save my boy.

"He was never yours. You must stop. The witch has used a spell."

I fought for a few more moments before the words sunk in. It was a spell. I didn't have a boy. I would never have a boy with Vincent.

Crumbling to the floor, sobs wracked my body. Durga curled up inside me. Her sorrow was my own for a moment longer, and then reason saw its way through. The witch was playing games with us. With Durga and me.

She used the cruellest trick of them all.

"Let us end this now," I spoke out loud, but my words were for Durga only.

She rose again. This time she put her sword in my hand and threw us down the tunnel. No more.

CHAPTER SEVENTEEN

I pushed my legs faster, flashlight in one hand and sword in the other. The sword was heavier than my knife, but the grip fit perfectly in my hand. My arms swung, lengthening my stride, I could feel the darkness trying to recede, but I was catching up.

I heard screams and yells, but ignored them and continued. I could not let her stop me this time.

Finally, I slid to a halt. The blackness was so complete my flashlight was useless. I tossed it aside.

"You are finished here," I said.

"You can't stop me!" A voice screamed through the pitch black space. Magic welled around a figure, and I could make out an old woman. Her hair was a frizzy halo around her head. She wore dark robes that fell over her plump body.

I raised the sword as her magic spilled forward. The floor of the tunnel turned purple, and the magic ran like water across it towards me. Behind me stood the rest of the team. Whatever magic was coming, I was willing to bet it wouldn't be good, so instead of risk it, I leapt. From a standstill, I threw myself forward, blade first. I twisted in the air, lengthening my body until the end of the sword reached the witch and penetrated her chest like she was made of smoke.

Her scream reverberated as she collapsed to the ground. Her purple magic dried up and dissipated until I was standing in the dark again. The quiet click of a flashlight preceded a glowing light that filled the room. The witch lay in a pool of purple blood. Magic ran through her even in death. Her hair spread around her like a halo.

I watched her for a minute, waiting to be sure she was dead. Her chest didn't rise.

Singh huffed as I turned on my heel.

"Let's go find that stupid vampire," I said, dropping the sword on the ground. The steel rang off the walls and ceiling. Durga and I strode forward, past Alex, Vilen and Ninel. Durga's anger was not even close to satisfied. She wanted more blood. She wanted vampire blood.

Singh led the way through the tunnel, his swinging stride covering the ground easily. His tail swished back and forth, and a low growl rumbled from him. When we got to the hole I had fallen in, he crept along the wall. Someone behind me was holding the flashlight, and it never faltered illuminating the path for me. I slid across the ledge, careful not to slip, then marched on. We passed the place where the birds had attacked us. Some of them remained on the ground, a few still flapping as if they could escape. Now that we killed the witch and broke the magic, the birds just wanted to escape the dark tunnels. A couple more fluttered past occasionally as we finally made it back out to the main tunnel. Someone flicked the flashlight off as we stepped into the well-lit mainline.

Durga was still steaming mad as she sat down between the steel tracks and crossed her legs. In an instant, we were both before Shiva.

* * *

A hot breeze blew through the open windows of his temple. The floor was sandy beneath my crossed legs, and the scent of bitter incense hung in the air.

"Hello," Shiva said, looking calm and relaxed. He was the exact opposite of Durga right now. The scowl on her face and the heavy rise and fall of her chest reminded me of a bull ready to charge. Her arms spread around her like a windmill, each holding one of her gifts. She prepared for battle. I pitied any stray vampire that got in our way. Vernon had little hope once we caught him.

"We must find the vampire," Durga scowled.

"That is your job, not mine," Shiva replied, coolly.

Her eyes narrowed, and she stared at him in silence for a moment. His eyes shifted towards her, and he picked at his fingernail. It looked like a nervous habit, but one I had never seen before. I sat quietly observing their interaction.

"You will do this, Shiva," she growled.

"It is not my place."

"I do not care if it is your place. I must finish this. It has gone on too long!"

Shiva sighed heavily and closed his eyes. I saw an image in my mind of Vernon in a tunnel. He was drinking from a man. A woman lay dead at his feet. Then the vision was gone.

"Are you happy now?" he asked, looking thoroughly put out.

Durga didn't reply.

* * *

A moment later, I found myself back in the tunnels, sitting between the tracks.

She pushed me to rise and then to run. The team followed behind me, but Singh ran at my side—at our side, because Durga was so close now, I couldn't tell who was in control. The pull from up ahead was getting stronger. Something was drawing me forward. My feet pounded the cement in time with my heart. The tunnel fell away and my senses spread out. I saw the tunnels as a map, and each section was lit up like blue rivers in front of me. I felt the tug pulling me and doubled my speed.

Up ahead the tunnel curved to the right, leaving a blind corner, but I didn't slow down until I rounded the curve and felt the pull to my left.

I slid to a stop and backtracked to the entrance of a tunnel. This one was lit dimly, and I knew it led to the vampire I was hunting.

I walked forward, my eyes adjusting to the lower light. I heard a rustling noise; It sounded far away, like an echo. The guys walked behind me, but the sound of knives and swords unsheathing confirmed they had heard the noise too. Lights dotted the tunnel about every fifty feet, leaving long sections in darkness before the next light illuminated the tunnel.

I made no sound as my boots ate up the distance between lights. I could feel them all now. There was more than a couple, so many I couldn't count them.

A hiss sizzled on the air, reaching my ears. My blade arrived in my hand, arming me for what I knew would be a battle. The vampires down this tunnel were not rogues; they were fallen. The witch's magic must have been hiding them. I would have noticed this many of them in one place. Beneath my boots, something dark stained the ground in the tunnel. I didn't want to believe it was blood, but the air held a copper tang that refused to let me believe it was something more benign.

I stepped on something slippery and refused to glance down. Fallen vampires destroyed their victims. I didn't need to see it with my eyes. I crept forward, into the increasing sounds of the vampires hissing and spitting.

When the first fallen vampires stepped forward, the battle began.

A red-eyed vampire launched from the shadow towards me, meeting my blade eagerly before the mass descended.

They swarmed us, and the sounds of yelling and fighting filled the tunnel. I sliced through one vampire's neck and caught the sight of Singh tearing the head from another out of the corner of my eye. I focused back on the monsters surrounding me and slid my knife home into the neck of a tall vampire as another clamped his fangs into my leg.

I screamed, and my blade crashed down onto its head. It released my flesh and reared back to bite again as my knife slide cleanly through its neck, severing its spine. It dropped to the floor as a vampire jumped onto my back. Its nails dug into my shoulders, tearing through my coat and skin, but in an instant, Singh launched himself towards me, ripping the monster off me and pinning it to the ground before tearing out its throat.

Blood sprayed in an arc, coating my face and blinding me for a moment.

I reached up to clear my eyes as someone grabbed me from behind, lifting me off my feet. I swung my arm down towards my attacker blindly, making some impact, but not enough to escape the steely grip. I continued to stab behind me as something carried me away from the mayhem and sounds of fighting.

"Lark!" I heard someone call. Durga rose and attempted to free us, but the arms were strong and determined. Singh's roar bellowed through the tunnel, but it made my captor move faster. I switched my knife to my left hand and stabbed that side too, but it was no use. The vampire who had me in his grasp was hanging on for dear life, and the sounds of the violence faded away. I yelled and twisted, trying to get back and help the team but it was no use. Up ahead I saw a solid cement wall, but the vampire holding me didn't slow down. I called out. We were going too fast to stop. Closing my eyes I waited for the pain to come, but nothing came, and a moment later I opened my eyes to a dimly lit tunnel made of stone before they dumped me on the ground and the sound of steel bars slammed behind me.

I jumped to my feet and threw myself at the solid bars that now trapped me. Durga kicked the bars, sending the impact through my bones and making my teeth snap together.

"There she is," a menacing voice said from a shadow beyond my prison.

When Vernon stepped out from the shadow, I could hardly see any family resemblance to Vincent or his brothers.

Vernon's hair was thinning and patchy. His face was an ash grey colour in the dim light, but I was sure it wasn't healthy even in good lighting. He had dark bags under his blood-red eyes and glowing.

He smiled at me, and his yellow stained incisors were long and sharp, leaving no doubt he was a vampire. I wondered if he could even pass for a human. I doubted it. He was grotesque.

"You can't keep me here," I said.

"Sure I can. I had the witch make this special for you," he said, pointing at the back wall. I turned my head, keeping him in my peripheral vision. On the wall behind me were markings in Sanskrit. They were like the ones Durga read to open the way into Metro two. She read them now, and when she read the final word, I dropped to the floor, mouth open in a silent scream as pain split my mind and fractured my senses. I cradled my head in my hands, praying to Shiva for mercy for what felt like an eternity before my senses came back and the sound of laughter filled my ears.

"Durga is so stupid! I told the witch she would read it. Now you are trapped in here without her!" He laughed again, almost unable to catch his breath. My head cleared, and I looked back up at the etchings in the wall. It was only then I noticed the purple line of magic along the ceiling. I tried to sense Durga, but I felt empty. Whatever magic was in those words, the spell was powerful.

"Now that you are here, I can go find my brother and finally kill him. Your meddling was very inconvenient," he scolded. I tried to hear the fighting beyond the wall, but it was silent. I hoped it was just soundproof.

"You'll kill your own brother?" I asked, trying to buy time before he left me here to rot. I needed to come up with something fast.

His grin stretched across his face.

"That is the only way I can rule the world, as I was meant to. I will be king."

I gasped.

"You thought you had it all figured out, didn't you? That idiot that has been roaming the tunnels all this time, running his mouth, I heard him talk. Once I knew of Durga, I knew she couldn't resist following me, but she was moving too slow. My brother was a nice bit of bait for you at least. He will die as soon as I have power. They all will."

I kicked at the bars again. He turned and slowly walked back towards the stone wall. I kicked again and again, but without Durga, I felt like a kitten.

"Wait!" I called. He disappeared through the stone wall.

I kicked the bars a few more times.

"You might as well stop, you will just hurt yourself," Alex stepped out of the shadow.

"Thank God. Get me out of here!" I said, shaking the bars. They didn't rattle, but I was so frustrated.

"I can't do that," he said, looking at the floor.

"What are you talking about? Go get the guys."

He looked up at me, sadness on his face. "You took too long."

"What?" I moved down the bars as he walked away. I remembered that a set of arms had carried me through the tunnel. My mind struggled with the thought it had been Alex who dropped me in the cell. It couldn't have been. Durga had claimed him, and she healed him.

"I thought I would be in these tunnels forever. I made a deal with Vernon. I didn't have a choice."

"What does that mean?" I yelled.

He turned back around to look at me. "It means, I can't save you today. I promised him I would leave you here, and he let me live. My hands are tied."

"Your hands are tied?" I yelled, banging on the bars. "Alex!" He disappeared through the wall.

I listened, but the silence was complete. Turning, I scanned the cell. The back walls were solid stone, and the front was all steel. I ran my hands over the bars, shaking each one, trying to find a loose one, but they were all solid. The stones were the same.

I studied the carvings. They looked like someone scraped them in with a knife. The edges were sharp and square. I traced my fingers over them and felt a pull like someone embedded magic in the stones.

I turned away from them and surveyed the cell again. There was nothing to see in the dim light. It was just a box, not designed to be comfortable or even keep a person alive.

Collapsing to the ground, I sat cross-legged in the middle, hoping I could reach Shiva. I closed my eyes and took a deep cleansing breath. Slowing each inhale and dragging out each exhale until they were steady and deep. I counted in my head, trying to pull away from my surroundings and into meditation. The minutes ticked past as I emptied my mind. I struggled to stop thinking, just to let go. I realized that Durga had been helping me meditate all this time. It had to have been her influence as I hadn't struggled to reach Shiva once since Durga popped up in my life. I briefly wondered if the magic in the cell was stopping me from meditating too but had to push the thought out of my mind before it took over and I lost all hope of reaching deep meditation.

I focused back on my breath, and finally, I opened my eyes to the familiar surroundings of Shiva's Temple.

* * *

"Shiva, we have a problem," I said.

"Lark, what is it? I'm quite busy," the God said, petting the snake curled in his lap.

"I've lost Durga," I said.

His head snapped up, eyes focusing on me, and shock registered on his face. "Did you make her angry? She once didn't speak to me for 100 years," He said.

"It's some kind of magic," I said.

"What magic? Who has done this?" He jumped to his feet, tumbling his snake out of his lap.

"Mahishasura," I said, for it was not the doing of Vernon. It had to be someone with more powerful magic than a single witch.

Shiva stared at me. His snake did too, then it slithered up Shiva's leg, into his pants and disappeared.

I shuttered.

"This is terrible. She must fight Mahishasura or the entire world is at stake."

"I know the story," I replied, rubbing my forehead.

"Tell me exactly what happened," he said. So I filled him in about the witch and Vernon and Mahishasura, when I finished, he continued to stare at me. His chest was rising and falling heavily.

"So, they trapped you in a hidden tunnel below Moscow, with Sanskrit inscribed on the wall?"

"Yes," I replied.

"Summon your vampire to free you. Perhaps once you have left the place of magic, Durga will return to you. If not, all is lost. Go now!" he stepped towards me and made a shooing motion with his hands.

"Wait! What do you mean summon my vampire?"

"The one you claimed as your own. Durga did not claim him; you should be able to reach him."

"What does that even mean?" I asked, rising and trying to stop him from kicking me out.

"It means go, NOW!" he said, and suddenly I was back in my cell.

* * *

CHAPTER EIGHTEEN

The one I claimed as my own… that was what Shiva said. I was almost sure that meant Drew. He was the only one I had claimed. I thought Durga had claimed him though. Isn't that what she said? She got all Goddess-like and yelled at Vincent. Hmm. I didn't know how to summon him, so I sat in the cell and thought about him. I thought of him in Vaughn's mansion in Moscow, though I couldn't send out my senses to find him. I thought of him leaving the house and coming downtown.

I thought I could see him. I focused so hard that it seemed like he was doing it — walking out the door and getting into a hatchback car. Vincent was following him, and I didn't want Vincent to come. Or maybe I did. I was so confused by Vincent right now and my feelings for him. I wanted him, but he was being unreasonable. Guilt ate at me, though. I wanted to kill Vernon, but I didn't want to destroy Vincent's brother. I thought I could see

Vincent's mouth moving and Drew driving the car through the city at high speed. He banged on the steering wheel and yelled at Vincent.

I hoped it was some kind of magic because if it was all in my head, I was in for a big letdown when they didn't show up. I watched as Drew parked the car and got out. Vincent lifted a cover off a manhole. I didn't recognize this one, but they dropped into a tunnel and raced through the dark space until they came out into what looked like Metro 2. The smooth cement and glistening steel tracks were identical. They ran along the tracks and skidded to a stop at a tunnel that looked like all the rest, but I hoped it was the one we had turned down.

When they came upon a bunch of dead vampires, I knew it was the right one. I tried to see if Vilen or Ninel were there, but I didn't get a good look. There seemed to be a lot of dead vampires though. A good sign, probably.

Suddenly, they stopped, and Alex strode out of a shadow.

"Kill him!" I yelled into the empty cell.

Drew pulled out a long knife, and I saw Alex's hands go up. Vincent grabbed him by the throat and looked back at Drew. I could see Drew struggling with what he was doing as if he wasn't sure why he was holding his weapon.

Alex pointed down the tunnel, the look on his face was pleading. Vincent had his look of pure rage that I had seen a few times. He threw the smaller vampire down the tunnel in the opposite direction and then he and Drew ran again, heading toward my hidden tunnel.

My legs had gone numb from sitting cross-legged so long, but I knew they would arrive soon and I had to make sure they came through the wall.

They got the end of the tunnel and stopped. I imagined Drew walking through the wall. He stared at it like it was crazy. His brow lowered as he inspected the stones. I watched him reach out and try to place his hand on the wall, his fingers fell through, and then he lurched forward.

I opened my eyes to find him at the bars in front of me a moment before Vincent.

Drew smiled and looked down at me. "Did you use some crazy magic?"

I bit my lip. "Yeah, I guess so. I need a little help to get out of here. It's spelled."

Drew pulled on the bars and then turned and kicked them like I had been doing. He was stronger than I was without Durga though, so when he kicked it, stone dust fell, and the bar rattled. He kicked it several more times as Vincent stared at me. I kept my eyes on Drew and tried not to meet Vincent's eyes. Things were weird between us right now. I didn't like it.

Finally, the bar Drew had been kicking gave way. I jumped up and slipped through the small opening. It was still a tight squeeze, and I would probably have a bruise on my chest, but I made it out and then grabbed Drew's hand and pulled him back through the hidden doorway into the tunnel.

Durga's scream of rage was deafening as she flooded back into me. She filled every part of me like I was too small. My skin pulled and finally my arms split, and I became Durga.

Vincent found himself held against the wall by the throat. Apparently, we were blaming Vincent for the trouble his brother made for us.

"You will stay out of my way. There is no hope for the vampire you once called brother. He will die today, and if you stand in my way, you will die too!" Her voice was low and barely controlled but echoed through the tunnel like thunder.

If I had been on the receiving end of that rage, I would have probably died from the threat alone. Vincent turned his head, exposing his neck to her, and she dropped him to the floor where he coughed and sputtered.

Durga turned her back on Vincent, Drew's eyes were wide, and she strode forward.

"You are a good and loyal warrior in my war. We must find Ninel and Vilen, and then we fight."

"When you finish, do not return to my city, I will not try to stop you, but do not follow me," Vincent said from the ground where he still sat. His eyes met mine and Durga snorted at him.

"You think I need your permission to go where I please?" her glare burned into him.

"No, Goddess," he muttered.

She turned and strode down the tunnel, leaving Vincent on the ground. Drew's feet followed along behind as she sent out our senses and found Ninel, Vilen and Singh. Those who were hers.

I wanted to look back at Vincent. I tried to force my head to look back, but Durga was too angry. She kept our eyes locked forward, but she softened the further we got from him. Finally, she let go of control, my body returned to my shape, but we were too far, I didn't bother looking back. What was the point anyway? He didn't want me to return to his home. We would kill his brother and then that would be that.

"It will be fine Lark," Drew said. His voice startled me from my thoughts.

"It probably won't, but it is what it is."

He nodded, and we continued in silence. Durga pushed me down the main tunnel to another one where Vilen and Ninel were. Singh bounded up and rubbed his face across my stomach.

"I am sorry, Goddess." Ninel fell to his knees and bowed his head. Vilen followed suit.

"It's OK guys. You kind of had your hands full, let's just go, all right?"

They got to their feet, and I turned back to leave, but the giant tiger wouldn't stop weaving in front of me and rubbing on my chest.

"Singh, we need to move. I need to get Vernon before he leaves the country."

Singh's purr rattled through his chest, and he finally relented and walked along beside me. We got back to the main line, and Durga pushed me into a run. I let my legs pump as fast as they could. Running was better than thinking.

I could think about how ruined my life was later. For now, Durga was sending me after Vernon.

When my knife flashed into my hand, and I came to a stop, I knew it was time to do what I had to.

"Come out," my voice called down the tunnel.

Movement along the wall was the only warning before a body slammed into me, taking me to the ground. Behind me, I heard the sounds of battle start again. It was almost incomprehensible that more vampires lived in these tunnels. The team had already killed dozens on two occasions. Now there were more. The stories of a city beneath the city must have come from these fallen and rogue vampires who occupied this secured tunnel.

I focused on my fight and struggled to get my hand out of Vernon's tight grip. He was sitting on my chest, holding my hands above my head. I dropped my knife and finally fought one hand out from his grasp, calling my knife back to my hand before attempting to stab the vampire in the neck. He threw himself backwards, and I leapt to my feet. Diving forward, I tried to stab him again. His fist collided with my face, slamming my head backwards, but Durga blocked the pain. The punch knocked out the vision in my left eye, but I could still see well enough.
Durga brought forth her sword. It was much heavier than my blade. The first swing nicked Vernon's chest but, like a fallen vampire, he didn't even notice. His teeth bared, he charged back in before I could swing the blade back towards him. His teeth latched onto my collarbone, just

below my jugular. His bite was so strong, the bone fractured and I screamed at the loud crack sound.

Durga couldn't stop all the pain, so she took over. Calling our knife back to my hand, she used it to slash at the vampire, getting ever closer to his neck. He grabbed the knife and pinned it down as he bit again and again at my throat. Finally, Durga broke my arm free of his grasp and used my hand to tear at his neck. I felt hot blood pour over my writs as my hand wrapped around something hard and sharp and pulled.

Vernon's body went limp over me, crashing down and knocking the wind from my lungs. It took a moment for my mind to catch up and realize I had just broken his neck with my bare hands. Or rather, Durga had.

Vomit swelled up my throat. I attempted to swallow it down and push the dead vampire off me, but his weight pressed hard and the vomit spilled up. I sealed my lips and thankfully someone tore the dead weight off me before it was too late. I rolled over and spewed all over the cement floor of the tunnel.

I looked behind me to find Singh shaking Vernon's dead body. The lion's teeth clamped onto the vampires already ruined neck, and his limp arms and legs flopped across the floor. I looked away before fresh sick could climb my ravaged throat. I raised my hand to my shoulder as my collarbone snapped back into place. Looking up, I found the team working effortlessly to destroy the remaining fallen vampires.

It was as if Drew had always been part of Ninel and Vilen's team. They watched each other's backs and fought seamlessly. Soon the last vampire fell, and the tunnel grew silent.

A slow clap came from behind me. Singh dropped his rag toy and let out a low growl. I spun on my heel, coming face to face with a man, except he had horns on his head. His eyes were glowing green, and his nostrils flared with each breath.

Durga rose dividing my arms and bringing forth all her weapons at once. She pushed me out of the way.

"I killed you," she hissed.

The beast before me was Mahishasura, Durga saw him as I did, but flashed the sight of him as a buffalo into my mind. As a buffalo, he stood much taller. Like Singh, he grew when he shifted.

Mahishasura laughed at Durga's words. "You think you are the only one who can return?"

Singh launched himself from the ground behind me, and in an instant, the giant buffalo Durga showed me, was standing in front of me. His great horns lowered, and he slammed into Singh, impaling him. Singh's roar deafened me a moment before the buffalo threw him into the wall of the tunnel. The lion slid down to the ground to lay still.

The buffalo shifted back into a horned man, but now he wore a cruel smile.

"I'll see you in the homeland," Mahishasura said, laughing. Durga threw her weapons at the beast, but before they reached him, he disappeared. All her weapons clattered to the cement. Durga let out a bellow of rage and then disappeared back to her space inside me. Her fury still tangible and making my blood course through my veins faster than usual.

I ran to Singh and fell to my knees beside him. Running my hands over his fur to check for injuries. The buffalo horns had gored him. A trickle of blood leaked from small cuts, but his chest rose and fell in a steady rhythm. I ran my hand over his thick white mane, and his yellow eyes peeled open. After a moment they focused on me, and he shifted back to a human form.

"You ok?" I whispered.

He gave me a cocky smile and winked. Little shit had been playing me. Or maybe playing Mahishasura. Perhaps it was better the Buffalo demon underestimated us.

I rose to my feet and helped Singh to his.

"Lark?" Drew said from behind me. I spun around and faced him. "That was an ugly dude."

Typical Drew, stating the obvious. I shook my head and walked past him and the Russian vampires.

"What is the homeland?" I asked Ninel.

"India," he replied without a second thought.

I turned and walked on down the tunnel.

"Where are you going?" Drew asked, jogging to catch up.

I didn't know, so I didn't answer. Alex was still in the tunnels, and he had betrayed me, but I didn't care. Or maybe Durga didn't care.

I wanted to find Vincent and talk to him. Fix things somehow.

There had to be a way.

I wouldn't let Durga control my whole life.

CHAPTER NINTEEN

I traversed the tunnels in a haze. My shirt was blood-soaked and clung to my chest. It had cooled to the point it should have been uncomfortable. Although my body shivered, I felt numb to the pain and the cold. My mind was spinning, and I couldn't slow it down.

Durga had said we couldn't save Vernon, but she didn't even try to give him a chance. She said she would, but when the moment came, we killed him. I killed him.

Durga didn't want me to be with Vincent. I stopped dead in the middle of the tunnel. Had Durga done this to make sure that Vincent never wanted to see me again?

Suddenly I was in front of Shiva.

* * *

"Did you find her?" he said as soon as his eyes landed on me.

Durga popped in beside us and Shiva jumped back as if something had burned him.

"I am fine, husband." Her eyes swung from Shiva to me. "You," she said, her eyes narrowing. "Are wrong if you think I killed the fallen brother to ruin your budding relationship with Vincent. Vernon was deranged, and he had to die. Vincent will see the truth eventually though you should be thanking me. I have saved you from a life under the thumb of a vampire."

"Yes, you saved me from happiness. Now I get to keep going through my life all alone. Thank you, Goddess," I said with enough sarcasm to ensure she knew I was not thanking her.

"How dare you speak to me in that tone," she said in her usual haughty voice.

"How dare you take over my life and flush it down the toilet?" I replied in the same tone.

"Now, ladies, this is…"

"Shut up," we yelled in unison at Shiva.

"Lark, Vincent will see the error of his ways. He is to be the king. He will see."

"He looked pretty sure of himself when he told us never to come back again. That was my home! All my friends are there!"

"He can't stop us. We will return once we have slain Mahishasura and he will welcome us."

"He won't!"

"You still have your Warlock," she countered.

I threw my hands up and turned away from her. It didn't matter, anyway. This whole discussion was ridiculous. Vincent wasn't mine. Neither was Frankie. My life was killing vampires, and that was all. I would be alone forever because that was the life they handed me. Everyone close to me died. It was better this way.

The sneaky smile vanished from Durga's face as I turned around, but I saw it. I knew she had read my thoughts. Fuck her. I didn't care anymore. I would kill vampires and forget about everything else.

* * *

"You with us?" I was lying on the ground in the tunnel. Drew stood over me.

I nodded and reached up to rub the sore spot on my head. I guess I could thank Durga for that since she apparently pulled me into meditation while I was still on my feet. I would just add it to the list of pain caused by the stupid ancient deity.

Drew helped me to my feet, and Singh rubbed his head on my stomach. Luckily Drew hadn't let go yet because I nearly toppled back over with the rough handling by my lion. I wove my fingers into Singh's mane.

"At least I've got you, eh, buddy?" His purr grew loud enough to echo down the tunnel, and I laughed unhappily at the thought of spending the next hundred years with my lion companion. I could be the crazy cat lady.

His head tipped up, and his fat abrasive tongue ripped across my chin.

"Ouch, you shit," I said wiping my face on my sleeve. That would definitely leave a mark. "Let's get out of here. I need to sleep for a week and drink a lot of good Russian vodka."

Drew nodded and turned to lead us out, but Singh's low growl filled the tunnel, and a figure stepped out from the shadows.

"Please?" Alex said, his hands raised in the universal sign of surrender. I tried to call my knife to my hand, but Durga, of all people, held me off. "I want to explain."

"Explain why you double-crossed me and locked me in a cell to die?" I asked, rage burning through my veins.

"It was part of the plan. It had to be that way. I had no choice."

I stared at him in shock. "You are trying to tell me that was part of the plan? You know what? I don't even care. Durga doesn't want you dead, so just get out of my sight."

"I promise it will all make sense, eventually. We will meet again," he called to my back as I walked away.

I strode on, honestly not caring. I wanted to sleep and drink and then go slaughter as many shitty vampires as I could find. This was my life. I would live it.

Back on the street, we were miles from the Red Square so took the metro back downtown. Vilen gave me his coat to hide the bloodstains on my shirt, but I still felt conspicuous in my hip waders. People stared at me.

A little boy across the train from me kept waving every time I looked at him. He reminded me of the boy in vision the witch had sent me. Elliot. He had the same soft hair and big eyes, but that was as far as the resemblance went. This boy didn't have Vincent's features or mine. He didn't look at me like I was his entire world. My heart broke a little more. I would never know a boy that looked like that.

I was still thinking about Elliot as we reached the hummer. I looked up to find Frankie leaning against the back bumper, his arms crossed over his chest, one boot crossed over the other in his classic bay boy stance. The look on his face was different though. Like he had seen a ghost.

"Hey, how did you find us?" I asked, but he continued to study me.

"Who is Elliot?" He finally asked.

Of course, he would pick up on that. Damn mind reader. I didn't want to talk about it yet. It was like a raw wound. My mind had trouble accepting I didn't lose my little boy because I didn't have one.

"There was a witch in the tunnel, and she used a spell to make me think I had a son."

Frankie looked away and bit his lip.

"What is it?" I asked, stopping in front of him. I wanted to curl up in his arms, but he had them crossed over his chest and didn't reach out to me. The team went about loading their things into the trunk and climbing into the vehicle.

"Had you just woken up, Lark? Did she catch you in between?"

"No, I was just walking down the tunnel."

He nodded and rubbed his hands over his face. "He looked like Vincent."

I stared at him for a minute. He was acting weird, and I did not understand what he was… then it occurred to me.

"It wasn't a spell?"

"It was a vision. She showed you the future. Your future." Frankie pushed off the side of the Hummer and walked away. I watched him in shock until he disappeared around the corner of the alley we had parked in.

I didn't know what to do with that information. I wanted to chase down Frankie and do something. Say something. Instead, I stood in the cold ally beside the hummer until Drew got out and ushered me into the back seat, carefully closing the door behind me.

The implications were huge. Elliot looked like Vincent. Could vampires even have children? I had never heard of anything like that. It would be a miracle. Frankie must be wrong. The witch had used some weird magic. Even as I tried to convince myself it was all just a spell and not some vision of the future, my heart cried out for my sweet little boy.

Tears welled in my eyes and blurred my vision. Singh's arm came around my shoulders, and I turned my face into his chest as sobs wracked my body. I cried for my boy and a bit for Vincent. The stupid vampire was under my skin and the idea we would have a son someday. A beautiful boy with soft eyes and so much innocence — it broke my heart. Durga tried to rise and steal my sadness, but I shoved her down and let every emotion pour out of me. She relented and drifted into her place inside me to wait out my sorrow.

When the hummer stopped, doors opened and closed, and I tried to pull myself together. I took deep breaths, but before I got it together, the door beside me opened, and Drew's arms slid under me, lifting me off the seat. I turned my face into his chest, and he carried me. I peeked back and realized he was taking me into Vaughn's mansion. The guys had already gone ahead in, and Singh was back in lion form, swaggering along beside us like a predator on the prowl.

"What's happened?" Vaughn's accented voice came from the foyer.

I pushed at Drew's chest, and he set my feet on the ground. Vaughn took in my face and appearance.

"Is it over? Is my brother dead?" he asked, his face serious.

I looked down. I didn't want to be the person to tell him I had killed his brother. I was sure he would take it the same way Vincent had and reject me, kick me out of his house.

He scooped me up in his arms and swung me around. "Thank you, Durga, for freeing my brother from his pain."

I tried to look at him, and he set my feet down. My confusion must have shown.

"He was a good man and a gentle soul before he fell. He tried to lead us all on the right path," he said. A tear fell from his eye, and he smiled sadly. "He was a good man. I am glad he is finally free."

"Is Vincent here?" I asked. Not sure what to say to Vaughn. His reaction was unexpected.

"My brother stopped by to say goodbye and then left for home about an hour ago," he said.

I nodded and moved to go up the stairs. Drew had gone that way, I wanted to find a bed and sleep in it for a few days.

"He will come around," Vaughn said from behind me. I stopped my foot on the first step and looked back at him. Vaughn blinked at me with the same eyes as Vincent; as Elliot. I felt a stab in my chest at the thought. I took a deep breath and smiled at Vaughn though I didn't feel happy. I didn't want to rest all my hopes and dreams on one vampire. It was too much, but if that witch had shown me the future, Vincent would have to forgive me someday. I climbed the stairs and followed the sound of my lion snoring to a bedroom with a big plush bed. I hoped it was a spare room and Singh hadn't just stolen someone's room as I kicked off my shoes.

I peeled off Vilen's jacket and my bloody T-shirt. My sports bra wasn't too disgusting, but my pants had to go. My broken leg had soaked my pants with blood. I grabbed the first thing I found in the closet and took a shower. It was harder than I imagined scrubbing the dried blood off my skin as tears blinded me. The clothes from the closet turned out to be a giant sweater, I pulled it on and crawled into bed with Singh, curling into his warm back. I couldn't sleep, but laying down with my eyes closed felt good. My muscles ached, but mostly my heart. What a ridiculous life I was living. After about an hour of watching Singh twitch in his sleep, I got up. There were no pants in the closet that would fit me, but the sweater hung almost to my knees. I could apologize to whoever owned the sweater I had stolen, but the size suggested I was in Vilen or Ninel's. I had met no other vampires as big as them here.

I wandered through the house towards the kitchen. Several vampires were in the dining room as I went by, but when I walked into the kitchen, Kelly was the only one around.

"Oh, you look like shit," she said. I felt like shit, so it wasn't a surprise. I laughed though. The laughter soon turned to sobs and her thin arms wrapped around my shoulders. I cried on her shoulder for several minutes as she rubbed my back.

"It will be ok, Lark," she whispered when my sobs turned to sniffles.

"I'm sorry," I said, straightening and noticing the tear stains I had left on her shoulder. Shit. "I'm sorry."

"Don't worry about it. Why don't we get out of here? You could probably use a drink." I think I loved Kelly at that moment. She picked out some clothes for me and shoved me toward a shower. I hadn't done a great job in the first shower, so I took my time and got clean, washing my hair and then brushing it too. I put on a cute tight dress and heels. Not my typical clothes, but I wasn't feeling my typical self anymore. I wanted to be someone else for one night.

When Kelly stopped her car in front of a nightclub with music pounding, I knew I loved her. No guessing this time.

We walked in, and eyes followed us. We nearly matched in our outfits. The fog of sadness faded. A few drinks later, I forgot my sadness completely. I danced and drank the night away. Feeling young and normal. Durga left me alone, but I felt her sadness under the surface occasionally when I was too sober. A few more drinks and I forgot all about Durga too.

By the time the club was closing, Kelly and I were laughing and chatting with some cute Russian men. Well, Kelly was talking, I was ogling and didn't hide it.

"Lark," a voice said behind me. I froze. I knew the voice and knew, deep down in my bones, something had happened, and I wouldn't like it.

I turned to look at Drew's serious face. Singh and Ninel stood behind him.

I considered making a run for the ladies' room so they couldn't say the words I didn't want to hear.

Too late, he was right in front of me.

"They are reporting the slaughter of an entire village," he said. Ruining my night completely and bringing me back to the real world. I looked at Kelly. She was still talking with the Russians. Laughing. Oblivious. Her life was so much simpler. I wished for her life.

I walked back over and said goodbye.

She hugged me and told me to be careful. I turned back to the team.

"All right, let's go to India," I said.

At least it would be hot there.

The End

Cover designed by Kudi-design

Jen Pretty
Visit my website at www.jenprettyauthor.com

Printed in the United States of America

First Printing: Jan 2019
Name of Company

ISBN-9781775290667